1st Ed
£1-00

DAWN CHORUS

Beyond a shattering war lay a danger no-one had realised—neither the vast computer that had successfully foreseen nuclear devastation, nor the brilliant technicians who had built it.

In one night the uncertainty of a Europe in which Imperialist decadence mixed uneasily with a new liberal philosophy disappeared, as did the coexistence of the two superpowers at the mercy of a runaway technology and third-world saboteurs.

Teld Richmond, cyberneticist, found himself trapped between the machine that wanted his mind and a woman schooled for success in all but personal fulfilment. From this emerged a new human being, one who could view the imminent destruction of its race and decide without compassion whether it should survive.

DONALD J. GARDEN

DAWN CHORUS

LONDON
ROBERT HALE & COMPANY

First published in Great Britain 1975

ISBN 0 7091 5144 6

Robert Hale & Company,
Clerkenwell House,
45/47 Clerkenwell Green,
London EC1R 0HT.

PRINTED IN GREAT BRITAIN BY
BRISTOL TYPESETTING CO. LTD.
BARTON MANOR - ST. PHILIPS
BRISTOL

ONE

THE DAY was perfect for driving. Skimming over the road in his aircar, Teld looked out at the passing countryside and felt the usual urge to veer his car off the road, disregarding the signals from the police beacons, and fly out into the world of fields and woodlands just beyond the barrier.

If he did so, a police flyer, alerted by the beacons, would immediately leave its station and follow him out over the countryside, till either the smaller and faster police car grounded him or—the more likely of the two possibilities since Teld had no off-road experience—crashed into a hillside or tangled the car in a tree.

Reluctantly he ignored the impulse and concentrated on his driving. There was relatively little traffic on the road this late in the morning, and with luck he thought he could be in London before lunch. Then, after a quick meal, he could run down to Household before they closed for the day.

This was the first time he'd been excessively late since he had started working for the home electronics firm, and he revelled in the illusory feeling of freedom it gave him. For five years now he had suffered early mornings, late nights, sacrificed weekends and cancelled holidays which in his view earned him the privilege of being late without worrying overmuch about the consequences.

His weekend had been spent on the Isle of Arran with a girl he had met there while on holiday some months previously. Most of Friday had been taken up with the journey to the small Northern coastal town where a twice-daily ferry transported men and their possessions between the small, beautiful island and the mainland. Once ashore, he had hunted down the address she had given him and reunited they had talked through the night about the things they had done and seen since they had last met. The next day she took him water-skiing and sightseeing round the ruins of Brodick Castle and with amazing providence it rained heavily the following day, keeping them both indoors.

At six hundred hours that very morning he caught the early morning ferry from the island and after a long drive at just under the legal speed limit he stopped for breakfast in Manchester, hoping to find a space in the motorail heading to London. But all the carriage space had been prebooked leaving him with no alternative but to join the steadily growing stream of vehicles bound south.

Several hours later the traffic thinned out and the countryside was replaced by isolated factories and their supporting accommodation estates. Gradually these in turn gave way to larger factories and rural housing developments which themselves metamorphosed into suburbs. Before joining the Ring he tuned into the London Traffic Control Guide and learned that Greater London had been closed to all incoming traffic while the police sorted out the colossal traffic jam threatening to choke the capital city.

Defeated, he swung on to the Ring only to discover a small fleet of American tankers had also come up with the same idea and along with a few hundred other frustrated drivers he had to traipse along behind them till they turned off the Ring, leaving the speed lanes free of obstruction. With some relief he continued on his roundabout route south.

Half an hour's fast driving brought him to the Household factory once he left the Ring and he gratefully pulled up outside the factory entrance gates, fumbling for his ID card and promising himself a long shower at the first opportunity to get the travel-tiredness out of his bones.

The guard sauntered indifferently over to the car and accepted his card without comment, returning to the gatehouse to check it. Teld watched him go, noticing that the security firm which handled Household's security had redesigned their uniforms again. They were always doing this to improve their public image though none of the staff in the factory ever took any notice of what they wore till it was changed for something even less well designed. A couple of moments later the guard came back to the car and handed him his card silently without making any move to let him through.

" What is it?" Teld asked, irritated by the delay.

" I'm sorry, sir, I can't allow you through the plant," the guard said smoothly.

" And why not?"

The guard looked at him steadily for a moment before replying. " Your pass is no longer valid," he said.

Teld fingered the edges of his card thoughtfully. " In that case you'd better take me to your chief," he advised.

The guard hesitated a moment, then shrugged. " Follow me," he said laconically, and started back towards the gatehouse.

" What about my car?" Teld demanded.

" Park it by the roadside," the guard replied with no pretence at politeness. He signed a receipt for the visitor then walked into the plant's grounds with Teld under strict orders not to stray. This didn't stop him noticing the transports parked in the yard with an ominous lack of insignia on their sides. Inside the plant white-coated technicians watched him walk by with the guard, then returned to their desks or benches or models. Teld recognised none of their faces. With an increasing alarm he searched for the familiar figures he would normally meet every day but couldn't identify any of the people working on the shop floor, and a numb helplessness slowly strangled the brief hope he held that the mistake over his ID card would be sorted out once he reached the security offices. He remembered abruptly that the security offices weren't even supposed to be in this building. Unsure of how to react to this Kafkean situation, he felt as though the buildings he once knew had been repopulated with alien figures who haunted the still familiar corridors like ghosts.

They eventually entered a room Teld had only thought used for office equipment storage but now installed with desk and a pretty secretary who announced them over the intercom to whoever was waiting for them in the inner office. She nodded to the guard, who opened the door and ushered Teld in.

A short tubby man with glasses sitting behind a paper covered desk examined Teld and turned to the guard. " Who's this ?" he asked.

" He turned up at the gate this morning with one of their passes," the guard replied.

" And who does he say he is ?"

Before the guard could reply, Teld stepped forward. " Teld Richmond, Assistant Director of Research and Development, joined firm as cybernetic consultant 1994—"

" One of their executives, eh ?" the fat man asked. He stared at Teld for a moment, then pulled a folder from a desk drawer and leafed through the pages, finally comparing Teld with a set of photos clipped to a sheet. He gradually lost his air of hostility and said to the guard : " All right Bradley, you can return to the gate."

" Very good, Mr. Kent," the guard replied.

After he had left Kent waved Teld into a chair. " I'm sorry I can't offer you a drink or anything," he apologised, " but you know what these government places are like."

" Government ?" Teld echoed, puzzled.

" Yes, I can't even smoke a cigar, the air-conditioning

system's out of service," Kent continued. " But of course . . . you wouldn't know." He frowned. " I'm sorry, but there's very little I'm allowed to tell you."

" I don't understand," Teld replied.

" Of course you don't," Kent sighed. " You no longer work here, that's all. If you want a more detailed explanation you'll have to get it from one of your own people."

" But what about my gear ?" he asked.

Kent held up his hand. " Don't worry about that, everything will have been left exactly as it is, with your personal files and notebooks untouched. You can collect them now, if you like. I'll ring for someone to go with you."

" I can find my own way to my office," Teld said.

" I don't doubt it, but nevertheless you'd better have an escort all the same. We've only just moved in and the guards will be making random spot-checks on people's passes. If they find you haven't got one they'll only bounce you down the stairs back to me again." He pressed a stud underneath the lip of the desktop and a moment later two burly guards rushed into the room, and straightened up when they found no struggle. " Forsyth, escort Dr. Richmond up to his office. He's called to collect some of his personal belongings. Then see him safely to the gate."

The man called Forsyth nodded and stood waiting by the door while the other guard melted back to wherever he had come from. Kent left his chair and shook Teld's hand warmly. " Sorry we have to meet like this," he said, " but I hope everything works out all right. I'm afraid

I can't ask you to stay longer but I've got a hell of a lot of work to get through as it is. Anyway, good luck."

Teld followed the guard out into the corridor and to the lift. "How long have you been here?" he asked Forsyth.

The man smiled. "I'm sorry sir, but I'm not authorised to answer any questions."

On the thirtieth floor Teld saw two guards standing watch in the corridor outside his office and in the reception room found a new secretary sitting behind the desk. She looked at him and then at the guard, who shook his head. "It's all right," he said. "He's been okayed."

He searched through the items in his desk drawers and found everything in the same state of disorder he'd left it Friday. What he considered unimportant he dumped in the desk shredder while everything he wanted to salvage he slipped into a folder or in his pockets. Kent had apparently told him the truth about everything remaining untouched—not that it mattered, since very important material was always kept in the wall safe, which he didn't bother with. He hadn't left anything in it and he doubted whether Forsyth would let him near it without Kent's express permission—and in any case, they had in all probability changed the combination by now.

"I'm ready," he told the guard, and they returned to the gatehouse. His car was still where he had left it. He pushed the folder into the small safe built under the driver's seat and then started the turboes. The car raised itself to medial lift, and one of the guards left the gatehouse to watch him impassively. He brought the car up to maximum lift and edged out into the road, carefully keeping the guard's image in the mirror and waiting for him to relax. When he saw the guard turn his back Teld brought the aircar round in a screaming turn and cut across the grass verge on a collision course with the wall. At the last moment he banked the car sharply away, bringing the full force of the jets against the pressure sensors embedded in the wall. Alarms took up the silence left by the car's jets as they died down and as he swept back out on to the motorway he pictured with pleasure the confusion he had caused.

By the time the false alarm had been cancelled, he was heading further south and running over in his mind the names and addresses of people he could contact for information about the Machiavellian happenings at the factory. The nearest address was that of his superior's, Dr. Reynold Hope's, Director of Research and Application, and now supposedly in the same position he was. Hope was the only top executive staff member Teld had come to know well at Household. Working for such a busy and efficient firm like Household left no time during the day for socialising and with the advent of aircars and rapitrans very few people in the plant lived within calling distance of each other.

Between sales talks, business lunches and progress reports Teld and Hope had struck up a relationship they both would have liked to extend out into their leisure hours but with the new expansion plans they could never find the time to set a future date. And now it had taken the unexplained disappearance of everything familiar at

Household to force him down to the town where Hope lived. Somehow Teld didn't relish the coming meeting.

The plant had mainly been concerned with R & D with a little area maintenance thrown in to save the expense of having another building set aside solely for that purpose. But driving along Teld began to analyse past events with what he knew about economics and finally wondered why the Government hadn't taken over Household some time ago.

Under the present administration's Modular Economy Agreement the various member-countries of the European Combine agreed to pool their monetary system into a common unit of exchange and limit their individual economic growth rate into a uniform percentage. This depended on firms within the economic framework keeping their expansion down to a specified minimum—and any firm exceeding this was ' merged ' with the Government while experts slowed or stepped up the rate till it fitted in with the rest of the economy, after which the firm was released from economic control. It seemed that under the MEA Household had somehow fallen afoul of the laws and the so-called Modular government had dealt with them in their usual manner, characteristically wasting no time at all. None of this would affect the shop floor technics while the executive staff would be ' released from their contracts '—and of whose number Teld could now count himself bitterly as one.

He turned off the motorway at Birling, leaving the London suburbs far behind as he penetrated deeper into the heart of the restored British Countryside. Hope lived in what had once been a modest little country house which had been overtaken by suburban expansion, but had still retained its existence due to the stubbornness of the previous owner, who defied council pressure to keep the house for his family. He sold the lease before he died to Hope and the council congratulated itself on having rid itself of one obstreperous tenant only to find that it had merely gained an equally defiant but infinitely more influential one instead. Rather than admit defeat twice on one property the council retreated to vent its spleen on other, more easily intimidated tenants. Being so strikingly different from its surroundings, the house was easily found.

The driveway had been laid in the form of a loop around a sculpture standing a few metres in front of the house. It was a carving of a boy riding a chariot of waves made by and drawn by two dolphins. The slipstream threw the boy's hair back into a long mane, and while one hand held rein on the dolphins, the other was held out in a half-pleading, half-defiant gesture to anyone entering from the drive. The water which poured from holes set into the dolphins' mouths into the pool around the sculpture seemed an incongruous and mocking addition.

A short brunette answered the doorbell. "Can I be of any assistance?" she asked. Teld could detect a slight Central European accent in her voice.

"I'd like to see Mr. Hope," Teld said.

"I'm sorry, but Mr. Hope is on holiday at the moment and is not expected back for a few weeks. Would you care to leave a message?"

"I know that Mr. Hope is at home," Teld replied, "and unless you make some effort in the next few minutes to contact him I'll return later with the police. Do I see him or not?"

The smile faded from her face—which was a pity; she had a nice smile and a pretty face—but before she could match threat with threat Hope entered the hall and nodded to him. "It's all right, Ines," he said. "You can let Dr. Richmond through."

The maid apologised and stepped to one side.

"Sorry about that," Hope said once they were alone. "I've given Ines orders not to let anyone know I'm here till I've had a chance to look them over. There'll be a lot of people coming round here in the next few days who've no right to disturb my peace and quiet. Didn't you get the message I sent to your flat?"

"I wasn't there this weekend."

Hope winced. "And you went straight to the plant this morning. It must have been quite a shock."

Teld nodded. "What happened? From what I can gather we've been taken over by the Government."

Hope poured them both drinks. "There isn't much to tell," he began. "Household collapsed as a going concern Saturday morning, though I didn't know anything till the evening, and then it was Sunday morning before I could contact any of my staff. This thing has been hushed up pretty effectively. The news media didn't get the news until an hour ago."

"How did it happen?"

"Well, we'd arranged to expand in what we had

thought were the limits laid down in MEA, meaning our subsidiary companies—without which we wouldn't survive—could be also expanded at the same rate as the parent company. Unfortunately, this ain't so—with the result that the Government moved in and took control on the ground that our expansion plans contravened the MEA. For which we have the legal eagles to blame, although I think there may have been a little collusion between those eminent gentlemen and our Board of Directors. However, there was nothing we could do except think how best we could land on our feet. We'd signed contracts with half of European industry to handle the expansion and taken orders with advances from the other half, in addition to the expensive promotion campaign and the negotiations for a breakthrough into the Pacific market. When they found out we were mortgaged up to the tax returns they screamed blue murder and charged us with unethical business practices. Us!" He shrugged philosophically.

"And where do we stand now?" Teld asked.

"Household belongs lock, stock and circuit breaker to the Government—and the only good aspect of that is they'll be absorbing the suits filed against us for contract breaking and nondelivery of orders. In addition to which we ourselves will be filing our own suit over the release from contract clauses. Now you're classed as an unemployed executive, wouldn't you like to join us?"

Teld shrugged. "I honestly don't know. What do you expect to achieve? You know how these court cases can be tied up in legal tinsel. You might live to see your money—if they cure old age. What do you do in the meantime?"

" Work, of course," Hope replied. " The Directors have picked up quite a few contacts on their way to the top. They won't lack for a boardroom table to crawl under. Come to that, neither will you or I. What with the war threat there won't be too much trouble finding a job in a weapons computer company." He swallowed his drink in one quick movement and stood up. " Dinner should be ready soon and you're invited. Don't be surprised, Ines eats with us. She's almost one of the family. In fact, if I wasn't happily married . . ." he sighed. " But married I am."

* * *

Teld returned to his flat slightly depressed and in need of a drink. While working, the flat was nothing more than a stopover from his office, with the occasional weekends spent away. Consequently, he had let things drift and he noticed that in the cold clear light of day entropy had established a beachead in the tiny flat. Recalling unhappily that entropy could never be reversed but only temporarily arrested he started tidying up.

His living-room measured only eight feet by ten. The furniture was set flush with the wall to give maximum space with minimum intrusion, and the spaces for books and the inevitable minutiae which small homes collected were in fact just slots in the walls. The television set was merely a honeycomb of cathode rays, each with their individual cathode ray replacing the cumbersome sets in use several decades previously, and the only controls needed were the programme selector and the on/off volume—neither of which had ever been used.

The kitchen was designed on much the same lines, with economy of space uppermost in the designer's mind. The cupboards were shallow but with carefully planned packing could hold a week's supply of foodstuffs. The double sink unit could just hold the soiled dishes from a family's evening meal. The cooker used controlled thermal planes to allow a casserole to be cooked next to rapidly cooling cakes. No single point in the kitchen was beyond the reach of a normally proportioned human being standing in the centre of the room.

The bedroom was but three walls round a bed which Teld judged to be big enough for two thin people sleeping on their sides. Yet despite the constricted design, millions in Europe lived under the same conditions he found almost intolerable. It was hard for him to credit that a family of four could live for long here without going crazy. The children's room in the flat was used for storage of magazines and suitcases but could be cleared to sleep one adult. His only original reason for taking the flat had been that it was cheap and near the factory. But now, with the time on his hands to appreciate the brilliance of the design, he decided to look for something less depressing.

It seemed the more coffee he drank, the less he liked the apartment or those who had built it. After overcoming a lot of personal resistance, he decided to spend the night elsewhere and find somewhere else the next day. He judged his savings could afford it. After all, the war threat would prompt computer companies to sign on top-line technicians. He hoped.

CHAPTER TWO

He was forced to leave his car on the outskirts of the city and catch a rapitrans to the station nearest the flatblock he'd been intending to visit. Since the closure of Inner London to surface traffic the old Underground had been remodified to cope with the extra passenger and freight loads it would have to handle if the city was going to survive as a functioning unit. To a certain extent the rapitrans, imported from America, solved some of the problems but the pride and joy of the Underground was the shop delivery system which kept small traders in the city supplied with stock.

Most of Inner London had been built before the birth of city planning and while the traffic ban caused pedestrian congestion and added to the transport overload elsewhere in the city it was the only realistic answer city authorities could produce to cope with the problem, the alternative being to completely rebuild London. At least the geodesic dome over Inner London kept the pedestrians moving whatever the weather.

The crowds, though, irritated Teld. He had never liked

cities and considered himself fortunate in not having been brought up in one, though this meant he was unprepared to face the overpopulated and confined environments found in most European cities. Facing the stream of humans from the station he could feel the faceless unidentifiable nature reach out to absorb him and strip him of whatever personality he had till he was just as interchangeable as any other member of the crowd.

The nearer he came to the City centre the more streetsleepers he met. Most of them were up and about, their sleeping bags on their backs and moving from window to window in the streets, or eating at the roadside cafes which catered almost exclusively for them. The majority of sleepers were students going across Europe singly, in pairs or groups sheltering under the geodesics which had sprung up over cities like spring mushrooms.

Towards the end of the 1980s streetsleeping became more than just a tradition of the homeless, but for some a pleasure, the modern equivalent of 'roughing it' on a campsite in the country. The police, however, faced with the problem of upholding vagrancy laws abused on a macrocosmic scale, issued licences to those who could prove that streetsleeping was the only alternative they had left open for them but then landed themselves with the problem of imprisoning thousands who were just seeing Europe. Regretfully, the police gave up their grand plans for identification control.

A few months later streetsleeping became immortalised in nonfiction books and several novels about the social and sexual mores of the phenomena. Streetsleeping became *de rigueur* in some circles. Canny businessmen saw an opening for a quick profit and manufactured small dens that could be made out of plastic panels which could be dissembled and carried around on the back during the day but would take just moments to hinge together and become soundproof, waterproof and opaque homes away from home at night. Inevitably, families found streetsleeping cheaper than maintaining the gilded cave and groups became polarised to form tribal communities. Before too long inter-tribal violence became too great a problem to be ignored and the police halted the production of dens and impounded those already in use. The rigid social nature of the communes collapsed and they drifted back to the loose collection of nonconformists they had been before.

But right in the city itself, rooted like some vast nettle, were those who had crawled under the geodesics from out of the spotlight, who built their homes out of cardboard and hid even further behind their impenetrable masks of hate and suspicion. Looking at these specimens sprawled in the alleyways, ignored and ignoring the crowd streaming by only a few metres distant, he paused for a while and looked at himself. After all, he only saw them from behind the tinted spectacles of prosperity, while the same spectacles seen their side of the line was coloured with poverty. And despite their common humanity they were separated by something more effective than light years from each other.

He hurried on past them, and a few glanced in his direction puzzledly before returning to the task of searching for what an overcrowded and under-resourceful world had left for them that day.

A few yards further on he slowed and sobered by the experience, took a fresh look around the crowd. The flow continued, hairstyles bobbing, fashions changing, faces too concerned with their own special problems to notice his inspection. People moved into his life and then, as quickly, out of it.

And after a few minutes he turned and walked back to the station, knowing full well he could never live here. There was nothing in the city that could attract him sufficiently to make him forget the hundreds living below his windowsills in abject squalor. The crowd surged with him, as though willing him back to where he had come from, but as he changed channels opposed him with incredible pressure, the action of hundreds of thousands of bodies operating in purely random ways. Even though he had his mind, his talents and his independence, the scene of a grimy child face staring out at him from under a shabby cardboard roof reminded him again and again that when it came right down to it, he had been just plain lucky.

* * *

Back in his flat he found a message waiting for him from some Miss Hunter. She had also left her business address and phone number. He noticed with slight surprise that the woman's address coincided with the city government offices. He considered throwing the data away, but from the answering service tape she sounded as though she had a fine, deep but not mannish voice. Although that told him nothing about her physically, it was strong enough to prevent him forgetting completely about her. He resisted calling her till after lunch, when curiosity finally overcame his resistance. The switchboard operator eventually managed to put his call through on a very busy line.

"Mr. Richmond?" she asked in her well-modulated voice. "Good afternoon. I'm so glad you called."

"What can I do for you?" he asked.

"Well," she continued, with a hint of caution in her tone. "It's rather what I can do for you. Is there any chance we can talk this over privately? Perhaps over dinner?"

"About what?"

"I'd rather not discuss it over the phone, if you don't mind," she said firmly. "Could you possibly meet me tonight?"

"I don't see why not," he said. "Where would be best?"

"My office would be best," she decided. "I have to work late in any case. Would nineteen-thirty be all right?"

He turned the proposition over in his mind. "Nineteen-thirty it is, then," he said—and hung up.

* * *

The young girl on desk duty directed him to the empty

lounge and announced his arrival over the intercom to his date. Teld was suprised by the offices and rooms—despite being Government owned they were far from the images he had dreamed up of draughty, bare-bulbed chambers. He sank into a heavily-padded chair and idly flipped through a sales leaflet lying disconsolately on the low table for the benefit of visitors. While he was waiting someone brought him a cup of coffee and after he had finished spirited the cup away.

Just on nineteen-thirty the door opened and Miss Hunter stood in the doorway, a slim dark-haired woman wearing a long gown that could be worn equally effectively in the boardroom or dining-hall. But it was her eyes which really set her apart from other attractive women. Deep liquid brown, they seemed to project her own force of personality along with an intense love of life. Teld stood up, unsure of how to act in such a situation, something she recognised and smoothed over with fairly inconsequential small-talk until the uneasiness between them had all but disappeared. She glanced at her watch after a few moments and said: "We'd better be on our way. After eight the traffic becomes unbearable. I hope you don't mind if we use my car—it's ground effect and licensed for the city."

He allowed himself to be led out into the darkening streets and to the underground Multipark. The car surprised Teld; it was sleek and feminine and *fast*. She expertly turned through the streets and joined the traffic flow out of London. Before long they were clear of the city and threading through the suburbs towards the countryside. " Aren't we staying in London?" Teld asked, wondering where they were going.

She shook her head, intent on navigating the traffic flow ahead. " Don't let it worry you," she replied. " Most London restaurants cater for the streetsleepers now. We're nearly there now anyway." With a burst of speed she brought her car off the road almost under the bow turboes of a surprised air car and in a few moments they were passing through a small sleepy looking town with old, respectable-looking houses, none of them more than four storeys high and the majority well under that. Once they reached the commercial district she parked the car behind a dimly lit, modest looking inn where they were shown to their places and presented with an italicised menu.

" Would you care to order?" she inquired.

" It's your evening," he replied. The unobtrusive decadence both amused and appealed to him, as did the impression it gave of being transported back in time to a style of living dead thirty or more years. It was a decadence, though, he enjoyed and approved of. There was nothing wrong with fashionable nostalgia, especially when it brought places like this back into vogue. Although he rarely had the opportunity to visit restaurants he wasn't totally unfamiliar with them, and neither was this Hunter woman, he decided by the way she talked with easy familiarity to the staff.

" Why did you decide to leave America?" she asked while they were waiting for their hors d'oeuvres.

He started at the question, then remembered she would have read anything on file about him before trying to establish contact. " In America I could only be one expert —however good—among thousands of experts," he replied. " Over here there's supposed to be plenty of vacancies open for bright young men in cybernetics."

" Ah, yes," she said. " But even so, you'd have still earned more and enjoyed a higher standard of living."

" But that wasn't what I wanted," he said. " It was too much of a cultural shock, going there virtually from pastoral Europe into California without having been briefed on what I'd found or how I'd deal with it. You'd have expected that things would slow down in America now they've allied themselves with the Pacific States. On the contrary—if anything, they're living at a higher speed than ever. In Europe, the Modular Government might be disliked, even hated, but at least it's brought the tempo of life down to a bearable level!" The first course arrived and they spent a few moments in silence while they ate.

" When you compare Europe and America subjectively," he continued, " you realise that there's a lot of differences which aren't apparent to someone who's never been there. Language, for instance. You don't talk about the burglar alarm in your flat, you call it the Home Defence Auxiliary Unit—the primary unit being yourself, with the gun in your bedside drawer. There are also a lot of foreign words which have crept into the language and over the years changed their meaning.

" And there's this situation, too," he went on. " No girl would invite a man out to a restaurant unless as an insult, or on a purely business basis. And even then, she leaves most of the incidental decisions to him."

"I agree with what you say," she said. "But the lifestyle in America could suit a lot of Europeans, while ours might be a correspondingly better environment for some Americans. After all, we merely made a choice between futures. Our sexual equality is based on twenty years' actuality while theirs is still nothing more than a professional convention. I might like to live there for a while."

"Suggesting tonight you're dominant through conscious choice rather than mood?" he asked.

Even in the low light of the restaurant he saw her cheeks darken. Then she realised she had been invited to relax the seriousness of the discussion. "I'm sorry if I sounded pompous," she apologised. "You're right. It would depend a good deal on what the girl wanted when she asked him out."

He kept the conversation from turning into a discussion until they were both relaxed and drinking coffee, when he was sure she wouldn't drop the closeness they had developed between themselves. She steered their talk on to the Modular Government in general, and he mentioned the collapse of Household.

"I realise that you bear a grudge against the Modular Government," she said, "which you have every reason to do. But I think I should be allowed to defend the administration I belong to all the same."

"Please do," he said.

"When Household first went into full-time production our experts ran a computer projection on the estimated growth, and decided that it was a 'safe' company. What we couldn't see was the rather predatory attitude of your Board of Directors towards the Combine. Then they submitted the proposed expansion plans and we found they were well within the limits set by the MEA. Unfortunately, these were later revised." She sounded defensive now. "We had little choice but to step in."

"Don't confuse me with the people who made those plans," Teld said.

"I'm not," she replied. "But it wasn't expected that you would suddenly decide to leave that weekend. Of course executive staff would lose their jobs, but you weren't executive and we wanted you for ourselves. Didn't you examine your stat when you got home?"

"No," he admitted, remembering that he had thought the only entry would have been Hope's hurried message.

"You should have," she said. "That's what they're there for. But listen. You'd be wasting both our time and yours if you went back to your old job. I strongly doubt whether you'd be happy sitting behind a desk and watching others design award winning circuitry while you polished cushion covers. On the other hand, we can offer you the opportunity of working with the most advanced computer in operation."

"Which is that?" Teld asked. "I've heard many claim that."

"The Oracle B-70." He didn't show any signs of recognising it, so she went on. "You may have heard talk about it some time ago. There was a lot of speculation as to whether one could be built. The ultimate in trend analysis, I think they called it."

Understanding broke his puzzled frown. " Yes, I know about it," he said. " But it would require totally new concepts in data storage, programming—"

" It's a well enough kept secret," she admitted. " There are in fact only three machines of this type in existence. The Americans have one hidden under the Rockies, the third's still being built, and ours is ticking merrily over in Sweden."

" You want me to go to Sweden ?"

" Of course," she replied. " You'd be be required to work in the complex itself under strict security supervision, but you're used to that anyway. And the nightlife is equal to anything the Swedes can offer."

He thought the implications through. " Very well," he said finally, " I'm yours. But will Modular be in power much longer ? After all, with the kind of money they'll lose through Household collapsing, they'll lose a lot of support they had among industrial leaders. Unless, of course, you've fixed the courts beforehand."

" What else," she asked coolly, " are legal departments for ?"

CHAPTER THREE

MEL—SHORT for Melissa—lay sleeping near him in angelic innocence, the blanket pulled half across her waist, exposing a long, slim but well-muscled leg. Despite his excesses of the night before, Teld had no hangover, and lay for a while enjoying the sight of a former deliciously voracious animal now stretched peacefully out on the bed, tantalisingly covered. He yawned and glanced at the clock, then sat upright with shock. It was nearly eleven. He hoped she didn't keep normal office hours, otherwise she'd be in trouble, but he still smiled. It had been a long time since he'd slept through this late on a morning, even with company.

Their journey home from the restaurant had been much shorter than the one to it. Melissa, showing a streak of low cunning he would have thought beyond most males, lived nearby in one of the nineteenth century houses, once all that low income families could afford two generations ago and now all that only high income individuals could afford.

He found a bathrobe and after slipping it over his

bare skin, ventured downstairs to the kitchen, which in this house was as large as his flat. Courageously recovering from the effects of agoraphobia, he examined the contents of the cupboards and drawers, and in just under ten minutes discovered the secret behind operating the percolator. A short while later he took two mugs of sweet coffee bedwards, left hers on the sideboard, and woke her with a long kiss. They moved apart somewhat unsteadily five minutes later.

"Do I smell coffee?" she asked.

He brought her mug over and she gulped the hot milky coffee down greedily. "If I weren't so tired," she said a few moments afterwards, "I'd tell you to go down and bring me my orange juice. What time is it?" She peered at the clock and groaned. "I'd better phone the office," she decided and slipped out of bed towards the door. He saluted her wise decision in not having a phone by the bed. She padded back a few minutes later and flopped down on the bed. "We'd better get ready to pack soon," she warned. "Our flight leaves this afternoon."

"Ours?" he asked.

"You don't think I'd be based in England, do you?" she asked. "I came over here especially to recruit you. This," she added, patting the bed, "is my decision. You'll be given everything you need to get inside the complex. But don't forget for a moment you'll need three times as much to get out."

* * *

The executive jet banked steeply to port and sliced through the dense white cloud into the overcast sky of southern Sweden. Teld could see through the window the sloping forests scudding by underneath to be replaced by the gentle undulating hills of Scania. Mel sat across from him, watching with an amused smile on her lips. "We'll soon be there," she said. "But don't be disappointed. Most of it's underground, and except for a few administration buildings and the accommodation areas you won't see much."

He moved back from the window. "What do you intend to do when we get there?"

"First find you somewhere to live," she replied. "Then I think we might see a couple of films on the computer to give you an idea of its capabilities. And a guided tour round the Complex."

Above the connecting door between the cabin and cockpit the ADJUST YOUR SEATBELTS sign flashed on. Teld buckled himself in to the seat harness and glanced at Mel. "If you've any bright ideas about conversation pieces involving air disasters, you'd better keep them to yourself," she said. It crossed his mind she might be afraid of flying, and that her groundcar was more than just something bought for a desire to own anachronisms. The plane began its final approach and they felt the nose dip and the deceleration pull at their bodies. Teld continued to look through the window and saw the ground come to meet the aircraft and flash by in a blurred green belt then slow till the blades could be seen singly. The plane taxied to a halt outside the control tower where they were escorted off the airstrip in a waiting car driven by one of the security guards.

As Mel had told him, most of the buildings were underground, but he wasn't prepared for the desolation of the complex. There were two tall, gleaming glass, concrete and steel skyscrapers pointing to the sky like white fingers in the distance, and beyond them a small group of houses. Despite the warning he still felt disappointed and cheated, though he couldn't have put down exactly what.

A class security card holders were expected to live in the Computer block itself, one of the two towers rising against the sky while other grades working in the Administration block—the other skyscraper—lived in the small, self-contained estate on the side of the hill. The rooms Mel had reserved for him were luxurious and much more important, spacious. She left him to pack with orders to report to the projection room at nine the next morning.

Dusk was falling when he closed the suitcases and slipped them on top of the bedroom cupboard, for want of anywhere else to leave them. Night fell quickly, and he looked out on the complex swathed in moonlight. Lights glowed fitfully in the village. Occasionally the tail-lights of an aircar moved down the road, or back towards the Computer Block. He realised after a while that the flight had tired him more than he realised. He turned off the room flouros and climbed into bed, surprised to feel that there was something missing. When he analysed the cause he shrugged it off—he couldn't expect her to fall under him every night—

* * *

The projection room looked very formal, and couldn't have seated more than twenty people at the most. Mel arrived considerably later than Teld, and before deigning to notice him phoned through to the lobby to page Dr. Fourneir. "He's the man you'll be working under," she explained after he'd asked. "You couldn't wish for a better chief. He'll be here in a few minutes."

In actual fact he was half an hour. He gave the impression of having been interrupted on a great and secret mission by the slightly furtive manner and hopeful, disarming smile. Small, harried and balding, he was very likeable. A pair of glasses with scratched lens were stuffed untidily into the breast pocket of his white coat. "Mel, my dear," he said, hugging her affectionately. "I thought you'd left us for good."

"You aren't that lucky, Dave," she replied, "and besides, I'm getting a bit old for globetrotting now."

He shook his head in disbelief.

"This is Dr. Teld Richmond," she continued. "He'll be helping you with the computer."

"And about time we had someone else to lend a hand." Fourneir said. "Welcome to Sweden, Teld. This your first trip?"

Teld nodded.

"Then you'll be a bit surprised by the social attitude prevalent," he said. "I think we've gone morally down since the Combine was formed. Besides, you'll be protected by the security from infection. It's a bit strict, but there are always week passes every so often. Some nice country round here. Shall we get on with the film? Then

I'll take you up to see our end of the computer. You'll have to forgive the quality of the film. It's been shown so many times if there were royalties it would be one of the most successful productions in the history of the cinema."

The screen flickered into life and over the credits a deep male voice introduced the film. "The Oracle B-70 computer," it said sepulchrally. A small table on which were set both terminal and visual display units appeared, held in the air against a silvery backdrop by the miracles of modern photography. The memory store and processor then floated in from the sides of the screen to complete the group.

"The Oracle B-70 computer is the most complex and advanced calculating device ever built in the history of man," the voice went on. "Developed by Dr. Robert Cynack in the International Data laboratories and draught-rooms it represents the first breakthrough in computer technology for twenty years, obsoleting all previous machines of its class.

"In addition to usual computer functions the Oracle can perform complex trend-analysis constructions, and coupled with the unique data storage techniques and interfacing programming enables the computer to give effectual predictions based on real-time events and situations. This capability removes it from the purely servile nature of computers and makes it the most useful tool ever developed by man, second only to the human brain. This facet of the computer will be better understood perhaps if we draw this analogy."

The scene changed and a cartoon caveman replaced the

table and equipment. " Let us consider the case of Clubb," the voice said. " Clubb has to kill in order to survive, and secure food for his family and himself." Clubb smiled broadly and waved his thick branch welcomingly over his head to the audience. " The only source of meat and danger to Clubb comes from, say, a herd of wild hogs living nearby." A surly boar materialised beside Clubb, who growled menacingly. Then they both disappeared and a view of a plain filled the screen. Clubb and his cavemates charged the herd grazing in the field. A few scattered but an unlucky number were quickly felled by the surprise attack. A small group of hogs turned on the cavemen, who beat them back with relatively little losses while they hauled the dead hogs back towards the caves.

" The question we are faced with here, is whether the hogs will survive or the caveman. On the surface it looks as though the caveman will, but taking into consideration the factor of time we can draw this diagram." The dead hog appeared at the top of the screen. " The hog litter is usually from three to five," said the voice. " Stabilising loss through mischance at one hog per litter per year, every female hog capable of reproduction—say, half the female hog population of fifty—produces four hogs per year, a total of one hundred per year, of which, say, fifty percent reach maturity—grand total of fifty hogs, half of which will be female, and ready to supplement the previous generation females now unable to reproduce. On the other hand Clubb, one of a tribe a hundred strong, can only beget one son per litter per year. Even though his chances of survival are much better than the hogs' per unit animal, his tribe will grow very slowly while the hog population doubles after four generations—and in that same time period the humans will only add twelve mature adults to their own tribe. Therefore—who survives?

"The information would have presented to the data processor before as two separate items for which he would have to make out two entries into the computer. The programmers would have to arrange two programmes to deal with the problem—not any longer. The Oracle B-70 will realise the situation for the programmer at any moment in time between the two antagonistic parties. With universal data input the Oracle can successfully perform the same operation with real time events basing its projections on past events. For the first time in history, Man can live out of his time."

The screen dimmed and the flouros brightened. Fourneir rubbed his eyes and refolded his glasses. "What did you think of it?" he asked.

"Fascinating," Teld replied. "As a technical film it leaves plenty to be desired, but from the layman's point of view I suppose it's adequate."

"Quite," Mel said coldly, bridling.

Teld wondered how he could back down without losing too much face while Fourneir smiled at his discomfort, before changing the subject and bringing them both away from an obviously tender area.

"Perhaps I should show Teld the complex," he suggested.

Mel nodded. " Don't give him too much to handle at once," she replied. " After all, it is his first day here. I'll see you both later."

Fourneir watched her go and shook his head. " People who try to make a fool of her usually find themselves in the end being made fools of themselves," he said.

" I wasn't making a fool of her."

" I know that, but she doesn't," Fourneir replied. " But that's between you and her. Come and see what this whole complex is about."

In the lift Teld found that the console floor-buttons were divided into columns of two, with a blank stud set in the space between the top two. " That's the button which'll take the lift down to the Penthouse, where the master terminals are situated." He smiled. " You'll see why we call it the Penthouse in a moment. But only the Penthouse staff—yourself, the other three members and I—are allowed there and to make sure no one else gains access that stud is fingerprint sensitive. This lift is the only way in or out of the Penthouse. Anyone who tries to force his way in will be buried under a pile of truncheon-swinging guards within moments. Doesn't matter which finger or thumb you use, they're all stored in the computer." He frowned. " I wonder if they've coded in your prints yet? Press it and find out."

Teld gingerly reached out and depressed the stud with his right index finger. No alarms sounded, and the lift moved downwards.

" Foiled again," Fourneir said.

After a long journey the lift stopped and the doors

slid open to reveal the Penthouse, which Teld felt sure occupied one whole floor of the Block. He stepped out of the lift and looked round. One wall was a vast glass plate, out of which he could see the countryside from a great height. He could see as far as the airfield where figures scurried round like ants and vehicles were just large black dots against the ground. The illusion was so perfect that none of the room's flouros were on, the room was lit solely by the light coming in from the glass screen. " How's it done?" he asked Fourneir.

" We've got cameras on the roof," said Fourneir. " What you're seeing is, of course, a computer construct of several views fused into one and presented as such. Just a touch we thought necessary if people are going to spend long hours down here without much hope of a chance to stretch your legs."

The floor had been carpeted in deep green pile and scattered occasionally round the room were bamboo plants in pots. In the geometric centre of the room was a large conference table, around which were placed chairs. Built into the wall opposite the vast TV screen were the terminals, with both line-printers and display screens. Progress lights blinked on and off in weird mathematical patterns.

" This is where it all happens," said Fourneir. " This is where we programme the computer—and it programmes us.

" What that instruction film tactfully left out is that we live in crisis ridden times, Teld. And the only way any administrative body, say, a government, can make decisions to cope with those problems is by knowing all the facts and in advance how those decisions will affect everything else relative to the central problem. Brussels depends on this computer for their policy-making. We also supply economic guidance, defence control, weather prediction and a score of other important responsibilities which rest on this machine.

" You'll find that the Penthouse team represents equally the different fields we have to work in. Rogov, for instance, with you is our scientific suynthesist, Leighton our economist, Michelson our Military strategist, and I the social psychologist." Fourneir slipped into a chair facing the central terminal. " From here we control the economic face of Europe, making sure that we don't let ourselves fall back into the cut-throat rat race the Americans and Russians have all let continue in their own countries. We also monitor the military situation and handle the defence of Europe. Did you know that Europe today has only nine per cent the stockpile but three times the strike potential of the United States with the use of this computer? The computer is patched directly into the radar cover and can deal with heavy MIRV assault while still directing our own missiles into enemy territory without suffering critical losses." He smiled thinly. " With the present political climate as it is it looks as though we'll have plenty of opportunity to make use of that. In some way it can be said that the war threat is an indirect result of our achieving independence through the computer."

" On the other hand, don't think we're dominated in

any way by the military. That would be like leaving a psychotic with a microtome-bladed knife. Totally useless having a special blade the way he would use it. The computer, as the film suggested, can fix near-future real-time events and to a limited extent offer ways of dealing with it. Only we can implement such ideas. The military involvement is very useful—it means that we get a large slice of the defence budget every year for as long as the need for one exists." He chuckled. "Hence the deep pile carpeting."

"When do you expect to be using it?" Teld asked.

"Strictly speaking, we're using it all the time. It's engaged at the moment on several different programmes and till any special need arises—this is, if you like, a war-room—we just stay in our offices or the coffee room. But before we can turn you loose on the computer you'll have to go back to school for a few days at least. We've our own language for compiling programmes for the Oracle, and we call it ALTAN, and for different uses there are different versions but like any other computer languages once you've learned the basic pattern you can quickly adapt to small changes. None of the existing languages are adequate for what we need. ALGOL, which as you know is for heuristic computers, performs complex mathematical problems on relatively small amounts of data while COBOL handles large amounts of data but runs simple routine operations. ALTEN has to cope with complex mathematics and a fantastically large data input. From there onwards it's just a matter of getting used to the computer."

"Before we consign you back to the school desk, though, you'd better meet some of the other Penthouse staff." He led the way to the lift and punched for the twelfth floor.

* * *

Leon Rogov was a tall, spare, high-cheekboned young Slav whose moody grey eyes seemed more suited to scanning the horizon for signs of Germanic invaders than reading computer printouts. After a few minutes of talking with him Teld sensed in the Slav a like spirit of damn the Stab, and go for the long-shot. Michelson, on the other hand, was saturnine and very conservative, almost repugnantly so. But his mind was as sharp if not sharper than the others'. "Our Descartes," Fourneir had nicknamed him, fairly appropriately, since he never did anything without a reason, however reasonless at first sight his actions might be.

Leighton, the economist, was a spry old man with long arms and a seemingly permanent wry twist to his mouth. Before joining the Penthouse team he had taught economics at London and claimed that the only reason for his move to Sweden was to help control a phenomenon which had formerly proved him wrong consistently.

The coffee room was reserved for Class A personnel who assembled in groups and talked shop or argued, holding their polystyrene coffee cups in one hand and gesticulating with the other. Rogov introduced Teld to Cleo Samura, who he termed the only sensible woman left on God's earth— " She hates computers on odd days, tolerates them the rest of the time."

Mel arrived, still strangely hostile towards Teld but not antagonistic, and sat among the group like a jewel in an oyster, surrounded by adoring tissue.

Naturally the conversation was mostly about the war situation. " It's all happened before," Michelson said. " And the powers concerned have backed down. You can't tell me any differently."

" They certainly have nothing to gain by fighting over us," Fourneir said. " But with Europe now politically neutral as far as they're concerned, they've lost a casting vote in world affairs. Neither China, Africa or Australia have shown the slightest interest in taking our place, and while I strongly doubt whether there will be a war over the situation we can expect heavy infiltration in our government in an attempt to polarise our attitudes. I don't think that the Combine's statement that it would not approve the actions of either Bloc in a future confrontation helped, either. You see where that leaves us— an unfriendly power to both sides."

" The trouble is, they don't realise this is a changing world," Leighton broke in. " Admittedly, we've seen their stamping-ground behaviour before. But then Europe was a gaggle of small countries, without even a common currency, let alone a common defence scheme, and no political unity of any kind whatsoever."

" The time has come when political arguments have to be backed with nuclear strength," Rogov added. " They're not just squabbling over our little continent, they're bickering over a principle. To them we're just what we were two decades ago, except not so independently-minded. They can't depend on an easy political victory, so they'll be forced to rattle their sabres."

"Doesn't it strike you Modular have acted just a little bit irresponsibly?" Cleo asked. "You certainly can't claim that the decision to consolidate Europe and re-purchase strategic airbases from the Americans exactly fostered good relations."

"Neither did the request that the Russians relinquish control over East Berlin," Mel pointed out drily.

"That's between the superpowers and themselves," Fourneir decided. "Things can't go back the way they were even just a few years ago. The European frontiers are down and down for good, and no amount of pressure from Washington and Moscow will put them up again. We'll just have to muddle along as best we can under the threat of imminent immolation."

"A fate worse than a fate worse than death," Teld muttered.

"You can joke," Leighton said. "I often wonder if Thor were alive today, what he would use for weapons?"

* * *

He returned to his apartment later that night and found Mel already sleeping in his bed. He moved her shoulder and she woke up with a yawn. "What are you doing here?" he asked, pleasantly surprised.

"Decided to volunteer myself for service here," she replied.

" Can't resist my charms?"

" You couldn't be further from the truth. With all the money you'll be earning you can buy me spring fashions and all the paraphernalia of young love."

" Love," he said, " I'll allow. Young, though I'd be prepared to dispute—"

" Insect," she said, hitting him playfully on the shoulder.

A long while later he woke in the darkness and shook his head to clear the hair from his eyes. The windows had been left open and a draught of cool air rustled the drapes. Through the night he could hear the sound of men walking on the tarmac and the occasional growl of a patrolling aircar. For a time he lay back listening to these noises, and thinking about what Mel had said earlier that night, about feeling as though the computer were enclosing her, enfolding her, and hearing it think.

That the computer ' thought ' in the human sense of the word was a myth which should have been smashed years ago but in the face of more advanced calculating machines had perpetuated itself alarmingly. He could understand how to someone who couldn't understand the mathematics the computer used in solving problems and the speed at which the operations were carried out, it would seem that the computer was in fact ' thinking '.

Yet this one took the present and the past, and mixed them to come up with the future. He wondered what it must feel like to look ahead, into the future, and anticipate events which hadn't been born yet. Even more so, what it did to a person to see those things materialise, step by step, like the routines in a ballet known by heart. The possibilities were endless. There must be thousands of ways to utilise that ability, to make money, or to manipulate the future of millions. And yet, this was precisely what was happening in the Complex. Whatever the motives—personal or humanistic—a machine was being allowed to determine the fate of a continent. And that machine was eminently more capable than the people who were programming it.

* * *

The next morning he was shown his office and he began to familiarise himself with the layout. The intercom interrupted him as he was attempting to discover how to replace the revolutionary new design in file-drawers once they'd been opened. Dr Rogov was waiting outside to see him. " You'd better send him in," Teld said, with a heroic effort pushing the drawer as far back as possible into the structure so that it would appear to have swung out after the lock had broken.

Rogov cast a look at the drawers and sat down. " Mind if I smoke?" he asked, opening a packet of cigarettes. Teld shook his head. " I'm the only one in the Penthouse who does," he continued, lighting up.

Teld glanced towards the cabinet. " So much for the revolutionary new design." he commented.

" Oh, those. Some bureaucratic idiot ordered umpteen thousands of them, and it took us two months to have them taken away. If I were you I'd complain to Fourneir and within a month they'll be gone." He dragged on his cigarette and looked at the glowing end. "I don't want to sound inquisitive, Teld, but I was wondering whether you've seen Holm yet."

"Holm?" Teld asked. "Isn't he the security chief?"

"That's right. Hard as they come. Obviously you haven't, so I thought I might as well make a few things clear to you before you do see him."

"What do you mean?" Teld asked, suspiciously.

"That this security cadre isn't just here to wait out its term before going home to the girls it left behind. There is a definite need for security here—well, that much should be clear. But I doubt whether you've worked in an establishment like this before. This computer and the design is invaluable, and there are plenty of people—not just the Russians, but the CIA and Australians as well, who'd like to have their own. Or if not, see that we don't keep ours. Just don't go out too often and listen to what these boys have to say. They know their business, and you don't."

"Did Fourneir send you?"

Rogov didn't reply, but stubbed out his cigarette. He nodded towards the drawers. "My secretary knows how to fix them. I'll send her down later. See you around."

* * *

Holm was a tall, greying man, somewhere in his fifties, who had once been athletically fit but was now running to seed. He scowled across at Teld over the almost uncovered desk with eyes that read " Young scientists have no business in the laboratory; they are only there because they have even less business elsewhere." Through the ground floor window he could see out into the car park, filled with ranks of security vehicles. There was nothing in his expression other than the calculating glare of the trained soldier.

" This," said Holm, touching a folder on his desk, " is all I know about you. Most of it is very impressive. You are very intelligent, not an oddity here. I hope your attitude towards both my work and my men will be mature and intelligent. We try not to interfere with your way of life, but occasionally the need arises for searches, and we hope you will co-operate with these without causing any trouble. I have done my best to keep the security forces and the scientific staffs in peaceful co-existence. I trust you will not upset that balance."

Teld nodded.

" Good. Now from your report I see that you spent some time in America. You were studying there."

" Only till I'd passed my exams," Teld replied.

" Did you come into contact there with anyone who had strong political connexions?"

" Is it important?"

" Yes, very. I know that you came away from America with a very embittered attitude towards the system there. For a number of years afterwards you were vehement on the subject. You understand we have to remain politically neutral, no deviating to either side of the line. We cannot afford it."

A plane drifted off from the runway. It soared into the sky and out of sight, but the noise came through the afternoon as a high insistent whine. Irrationally, Teld wanted to go for a walk outside in the sunshine, not sit all afternoon in this office, especially with this paranoid sitting opposite him. " Look," he said. " I had some very bad experiences over there. One of my friends died in a plane crash that could have been prevented—but wasn't."

Holm didn't look as though he was listening, or if he was, paying any attention. " All this is extremely necessary," he continued doggedly. " I would sooner lie all day, fishing on a riverbank. But here I am, with hundreds of troops under my command who must be constantly monitored in addition to a civilian population who don't understand the need for a tight security system. I'm too old to lock up my girls and frighten away the boys they flirt with, my ideal is to tell them the dangers and let them work their own answers out. For me it is always the line of least resistance when I deal with people."

" And when we have work under a threat as real as the last war, our loyalties cannot be divided. However you feel about the Americans, or any political system, here you are just an observer."

" I don't approve of war," Teld said.

" What experience have you had of war? Although the threat of death is always present, there is something else which counter-balances your fear. The comradeship you find in the factories, the battlefields, the homes and the war camps. The false war the politicians make on their enemies—who they assume to be their real enemies

—has dulled your perception. No one can say whether they are really frightened of the hydrogen bomb being used, since no one has much idea of what would happen if it were dropped. When was the last nuclear test in your lifetime? They are banned now, by international agreement. It doesn't give the politicians and the generals the chance to show off their wonderful invention, and strike terror into the heart of any peace-loving statesman. That is why the current threat is so important. The likelihood of war is much greater than ever before."

" Whether you dislike war or not, the nuclear bomb will kill you all the same. You know where the shelters are situated? There are three. One is for both the Computer and Admin block. Another is situated in the Village itself, and the third is over by the airfield. In case of war you should make your way to the shelter, and wait till after the safety locks have released you. They all have their own life-support systems, so you will not be too badly off.

" That is all I really have to say," he concluded. " I hope you enjoy working here, Dr. Richmond."

Teld looked across the unlittered desk, and stood up. " I'll see," he said, and left.

CHAPTER FOUR

THE PARTY was in full swing when Mel and Teld arrived. They were late, but that didn't bother them overmuch; the party was still in progress and would go on till much later that night, till the various fractions drifted away and carried the party to their own homes where it would flare briefly before dawn and exhaustion set in.

Someone had taken a cassette player and was acting as DJ while people danced on the lawn and drank under the trees surrounding the garden. The house they were using for the party was 'borrowed' for the occasion and the conviviality had overflowed into the night.

In the house there were people everywhere, in the hall, on the stairs and the landing. Teld finally found Fourneir in the lounge, surrounded by the younger scientists. His wife Gina met them. Dark and attractive, she was at a guess half Fourneir's age.

"David likes to include young people in his parties," she explained when told about the nihilistic offshoot of the party on the lawn.

Teld looked round for Rogov, but couldn't see his tall

lanky frame anywhere in the walking, talking, dancing and drinking crowd. Michelson drifted over and placed a drink in his hand. "How're you finding the work?" he asked amiably. Inwardly, Teld groaned. He disliked intensely anyone bringing the subject up at social events.

"Not too tortuous," he replied. "And very interesting."

"The party seems to be going very well," Mel broke in drily.

"You should have been here earlier," Michelson replied. "If we hadn't invited Holm security would have been round."

"Is he here?" Mel asked, uncertainly.

"No," Michelson said. "He had a prior engagement, so we got off lightly." He glanced towards the door. "Here's Leon."

Leon glanced at the people milling around the room, as if judging the temperature of the party, and finding it acceptable stepped in. Following him was Cleo. They went to the bar and poured themselves drinks, then expertly navigated through the crowd towards Teld.

"I though you might be outside," Rogov said.

"What's it like out there?" Michelson asked.

"Oh, a good deal more active and colder than this place, but still fifteen degrees warmer than it usually is this time of year."

Fourneir appeared beside them. "Glad you could make it," he said. "Enjoying yourselves?"

"It's a little hectic," Teld replied.

" Shouldn't worry, it'll quieten down later on. I follow the policy of inviting everyone along. Then somebody who's somebody is bound to turn up and make the evening memorable."

" How Wildean," said Mel.

" Master of the aphorism," said Fourneir. " Or was it epigram ?" He shrugged. " However, they don't write like him any more which may or may not be a blessing. Pity about the way he died, penniless in a foreign land. But then, he certainly knew how to live."

" I doubt whether that would have made dying any easier," Rogov said.

" It leaves fewer regrets," Fourneir said. " Well, I'll see you later." He disappeared into the crowd.

Rogov was looking out of the window at the perimeter lights dancing in the distance. " What a lovely night, carpenter," he said.

" What price oysters, walrus ?" Teld asked.

" War," Rogov replied. He swallowed his drink and poured himself another. " I wouldn't mind if the sirens went. At least the waiting would be over."

" You shouldn't think like that," Teld said. " After all, it might blow over in a week."

" Or it might not," Rogov replied. " And if it did, there'd only be another one in a matter of months. You can't keep a world on tenterhooks all the time. Sooner or later someone will say to themselves, ' If they don't start it, then I will ' and drop a bomb somewhere—anywhere, it doesn't matter where or on whom—and we'll all go up. That will be the end of it."

" I seriously doubt whether there'll be a war," Teld said.

" Unfortunately the situation doesn't depend on your doubts and uncertainties. Nobody wants a war—but whether they'll get one or not is another thing."

" War is a canvas you paint peace on," Mel said. " When it happens, I'll start worrying about it. Till then, I'll act like there's no tomorrow."

" You haven't lived so close to it for so long," Rogov pointed out. " Yon device can calculate the possibility of war, even warn us of an impending political crisis but it can't stop it when it happens. It's not just the politicians, it's the life we lead. We just drift with the tide, getting the specified amount of work done by the required time. There's so little life out there."

" The war'll change that," Teld said, patting Rogov on the shoulder.

" Let's go to the Penthouse," Rogov said.

" What for?" Teld asked, surprised.

" I want to use the computer." He put down his drink. " If we use an aircar we'll only be a couple of minutes."

" Can't it wait?"

" Why should it? This is important."

" All right. Wait till I tell Melissa where I'm going—"

" No time," Rogov said, marching towards the door. Teld glanced back to where Mel and Cleo were talking, then, biting his lip, followed the Slav.

The aircar brought them to the Block in under a minute. As they entered the reception area the guard on duty nodded to them but they said nothing till the lift doors opened into the Penthouse. Rogov switched on the lights and the pale flouros illuminated the paper-strewn worktops and untidy table. Rogov crossed to the central terminal and punched in a code-group. " We call this programme Dawn Chorus," he said. " Because the sirens will be the only warning we'll get of an attack."

Teld watched figures flash on to the display screen and dissolve to leave sentences on the screen. He moved round to read them.

After a moment he moved back. " It obviously doesn't think we're going to have much peace in our time," he said.

" Things are going to be bloody difficult," Rogov agreed. " Still, what can you expect? You let a small minority group get into power, doesn't matter what promises they make at the start, they'll always break or shelve them later on. World peace is always the first of them to go and it frankly surprises me why the electorate get themselves fooled into believing one percent of what the politicians tell them." He sounded bitter, and Teld felt uneasy. He couldn't deal with hate any more than he could with war.

" So what are we doing here?" he asked.

" Trying to protect a little peace of God's own acre," Rogov replied. " Against the flames of hell. Did you know that there are reports of nuclear explosions going back nearly five thousand years? I don't mean bombs as such. Siberia, nineteen ten, I think. There was a catastrophic explosion there. I've heard all the theories, ranging from small particles of anti-matter coming from space, black holes a few angstroms wide ploughing through the earth, even suggestions that some underground society who'd developed the atom bomb were using Siberia as a testing ground. There are mentions of nuclear detonations in the Koran. I doubt whether they're much more than manifestations of human superstition, or descriptions of what the writer thought would be the ultimate weapon. Well, they were right. It is the ultimate weapon and we've got to live with it. We haven't been given a choice in the matter. At no point in human history has there been civilisation living without the threat of war constantly at hand. Whether you fight it with maces or muskets or lasers people still die."

"You can't change that here," Teld pointed out. "Why worry about it?"

"Because I have to," Rogov replied. "Don't get me wrong. I'm not out to save the world. The majority of the human race can go hang as far as I'm concerned. I'm just worried about my little plot of ground and my friends and my own skin. Five billion people didn't ask for the development of the bomb, and it didn't just happen. It was developed to kill and that's the only use that the politicians can see it used for. Our reactors for providing us with cheap power are decades out of date. But our missiles aren't."

He walked over to the wallscreen and waved a hand at the patrolling aircar passing by. "Look at the millions we spend on defence every year. And what for? Guarding against an eventuality which can't possibly materialise. Years ago they tried to ban spaceflight because it was useless, or so they said. Well, you tell that to the cancer cases coming back from the radiation labs in orbit."

"You've every right to complain," Teld said. "But again—what can you do about it? Perhaps there will be a war. In which case you'll be thankful for every inch of radiation shielding over your head."

"But they've no right to start a war," Rogov shouted. "Can't you see that? Who has the right to commit whole populations to nuclear holocaust for the sake of a few petty sentences in a treaty or charter or whatever?"

"Tell me about the programmes," Teld suggested, trying to ease Leon out of the hate-filled rut his mind had settled into.

"There's nothing much to them. Just the first to determine the possibility of nuclear war, and another to initiate retaliatory measures against the aggressors. Whoever they may be. The responsibility of the shelters is in Fourneir's hands. He decides whether we sound the siren when he's sure in his own mind that there isn't going to be backdown."

"And the computer doesn't seem to indicate that a withdrawal is likely, at least not in the foreseeable future. The trouble with it is that the higher the proportion of significant data is incoming, the less efficient are its prognostications. Still, no humans could work better under stress so we're stuck with what we've got." He punched in another code-group and sat looking at the screen as the list of Soviet and American missile bases unfolded in front of him. " War is too serious to leave to the politicians," he said after a while. " But then we don't ask it to stop anything. We just want sufficient warning to give us a chance to run for the hills when it does happen."

* * *

Back at the party, Mel steered Cleo into conversation with Gina and returned to the lounge, but to her surprise neither Teld nor Leon were there. She wondered where they could have gone, especially this late at night. None of the bars in the complex would be open.

Michelson and Leighton were in the kitchen, moodily carving sandwich cuts from a chicken. " The last I saw of them they were chatting in the lounge," Michelson told her after she'd refused a chicken sandwich of formidable size. " That was half an hour ago. Have you looked in the car park to see if their cars are still there? They could have gone for a run around the complex." He glanced at his watch. " In which case the security patrols should bring them back soon."

" I'll go and see," she said.

She found Teld's car still parked in the same place but Rogov's smaller model was missing. She took the keys to the car from her pocket and settled herself in the front driving seat, with the dashboard illumination lending a pale ghostly green glow to her face as seen in the mirror. Experimentally she turned the turboes on but the radar warned her that she was too near other cars to move without causing serious damage. And someone had parked right across the tail jets. The whine from the jets died and she turned on the radio for company.

In time she left the car and rejoined the party. She thought she knew where they had gone. Fourneir showed her to the bedroom so she could use the phone there in peace.

* * *

In the Penthouse Teld stood at the wallscreen, looking out into the darkness and towards the perimeter lights, visible as an unbroken line of brightness.

" We'd better get back to the party," he said.

Rogov nodded and cleared the terminal screen. They walked in silence to the lift. In the lobby the desk sergeant was speaking over the phone to someone. Then he looked up, noticed them, and signalled Teld over. " Call for you, Dr. Richmond," he said, handing over the handset.

" Are you all right?" Mel asked anxiously, after he'd identified himself.

" Of course," he replied. " Shouldn't I be?"

" Well . . . I didn't know where you were."

" I would have told you but you'd wandered off with Cleo somewhere, I'll be back at the party in a few minutes. I'll see you there. Ciao."

" Ciao," she replied and hung up.

* * *

By now it had turned quite late and a few people were leaving the party. Over the noise from several cassette players she could hear the muted growl of aircars lifting. She drifted back into the hall and poured herself a drink.

Fourneir intercepted her. " Everything all right?" he asked. " I shouldn't worry about them. They can't get up to too much trouble with security around."

They came in and looked around. Mel stormed over. " Thanks very much," she said angrily.

" I'll go and find Cleo," Rogov decided.

" Just get me home," Mel demanded.

" Whose?" Teld asked.

For a moment she dreamed of screaming and breaking a bottle over his skull. Then she calmed down, and discovered that quite unconsciously she'd been clenching her fists.

" The party isn't over yet," Teld continued, " and I intend to enjoy every remaining minute."

She picked up her own glass and held it out for refilling. " Then if you intend to stay and get drunk I might as well keep you company," she decided.

" Drink for drink?" he asked.

" Done," she replied, showing her teeth in a highly competitive smile.

* * *

Next morning neither of them felt particularly well or inclined to start work. They lay in bed for a while trying to forget the outside world existed, but this couldn't be done indefinitely. They dutifully swallowed the hangover pills and waited for them to take effect. As soon as she felt better Mel left for her office. Teld merely put some cereal mix in the cooker to heat and measured the distance to the bathroom with his eyes.

When he reached the Penthouse he found that everyone else had been similarly affected to differing degrees. Fourneir and Leighton looked down on anyone who couldn't take their liquor. Michelson came in with a set jaw and eyes painfully opened. Fourneir smiled his timid smile behind tinted contacts and said as little as possible as quietly as possible. At thirteen twenty seven the line printer hissed into sibilant life.

News Agency Noram Presynd states two aggressors to meet at Geneva and discuss conflicts with view to settling current confrontation amicably.

Fourneir broke in with a sigh. "Looks like that's it, boys. Another wet squib."

Noram Presynd correspondent Mick Lannder (political correspondent NY Times) reports as follows:
President Hoolihan and his Secretary of State Dr. Jonathan Dasilva today left for Geneva in order to conduct high level talks with Russian Supreme Soviet over the political crisis which has threatened twice already to erupt into nuclear conflict. President Hoolihan's strong stand on American rights in Europe has long been his political rallying point on election issues and now he has gained

the President he intends that the strategic military bases held for generations in Europe should be returned to American hands. This morning demonstrations by students and left-wing groups outside the White House were broken up by National Guards as the President appeared with his family to greet the Soviet Ambassador Nikolai Kostoyavich. Several shots were fired from the crowd at both the National Guard and the group standing by the White House. It is not known whether the shots were aimed at the President or if right-wing infiltrators fired at the Ambassador, who were both rushed inside so that the National Guards could deal with the crowd using shock sticks, gas and sonics. Several students are now in hospital suffering from perforated eardrums after a sonic generator exploded in the crowd. The Guards arrested fourteen men and women but the weapon was not recovered.

White House authorities see Mr. Hoolihan's visit to Geneva as a chance to if not end the conflict, then at least ease the tensions which have built up these last two weeks over the future of Europe. Brussels still maintains that its decision to repurchase Soviet and American land behind European borders and request similar in both countries was not intended to precipitate political confrontation.

European consolidation of these past twenty years is seen by many as a threat to the stability of world peace yet integration of Europe into political unity has been inevitable since 1945. Gradual rise of anti-Soviet/American feeling coupled with the distinction between a controlled economy with lower standard of living and high growth economy with lesser distribution of wealth also Soviet trend of socialism from American viewpoint and imperialistic trend from Soviet viewpoint created much ill-feeling during first years of 'splendid isolation'.

President Hoolihan and Dr. Dasilva now at Geneva welcomed with Sovunion representative Mily Yhurovka (Origin Reuter)

"I suppose they'll want to drag us into a big zoned continent," Fourneir said. "Well, despite the computer's baneful predictions the heat seems to be off at the moment. Does anyone want to patch into the news channel?"

"What worries me more than ever is that the two powers have less to lose than before," Leighton said. "The nuclear device was considered terrible then because of the fallout. But now, with the safe bomb, stockpiles have been built up to their pre-1980 level."

The argument raged on for a while, till increasing work ended it. They ran some analyses on traffic flow patterns for the Paris City Council and kept one ear open for stray snippets of news. Various officials were interviewed and established their faith in the talks. The daylight began to go and several people went home. Michelson called in to ask if there were any further developments, but the answer was negative. Everything seemed so far and remote. The increasing quietness worried Teld.

CHAPTER FIVE

THE AIRCAR nosed delicately out of the Complex gates and cruised down the roadway between the hills towards the coast. The sun glinted brightly on the windows and chromework. At the wheel Teld looked out into the distance and saw the outline of the small coastal town called Vortstag. Sitting beside him, Mel was reading a book and occasionally glancing up to look through her tinted contacts towards the hills.

"I still say I'd like to go and live in those hills," Teld remarked. "Just the simple life."

"You wouldn't stand it for two days running," Mel said.

"One day I'll prove you wrong," he promised. "The trouble with our society is that it doesn't provide any reasonable alternatives between the struggle of everyday existence and the down-and-out life of the streetsleeper."

"So?" Mel asked. "I used to streetsleep—and it wasn't so bad. I had some good times, met some very interesting people and made lifelong friends for whenever I went back to the streets. Not all the people who sleep up against a wall are bad, in fact—"

"—some of them are my best friends?" he suggested.

She glared at him. "That isn't what I meant—and you know it. One day I'll take you round the cities with nothing but a sleeping bag, a packet of joints and a change of jeans."

"I'll probably get to like it," he said. "But that has nothing to do with what I was talking about."

"On the contrary. It has everything to do with it. You were talking about a lack of alternatives. Well, there you have two diametrically opposed ways of life, both of them offering reasonable arguments for their right to exist. Yet if you did shrug off your thin coating of civilisation, which whatever the writers may say isn't that easy to do, and went off to live off the land, you'd infringe both those societies by breaking the laws under which they live. Remember, streetsleeping doesn't break any laws. The one rule it did conflict with, vagrancy, has been repealed, mainly because it was invalid anyway."

Teld remained stubborn, "True, the city life offers competition without the built-in dangers of going hungry or being eaten, but it lacks what the outside can give."

"You go camping," she said.

"You can't class a leisure activity as an alternative as such," said Teld.

She gave up and resumed reading. Teld parked the aircar in the hotel grounds and registered inside before having their luggage taken upstairs to their pre-booked room. Once they'd unpacked they drifted down to the seafront, Teld still advocating the necessity of a pastoral lifestyle to offset the dangerously boring and merciless city existence. Mel contemplated pushing him in the fjord but changed her mind. They were out on his pass and she would have a hell of a time wangling a return without him.

They rented a cabin cruiser and oncc they reached the mouth of the fjord guided the craft a mile out into the sea, where they would be within range of the shore-signal but unbothered by water-skiiers and other tourists in cruisers. Teld disliked water-skiing intensely and rejected Mel's suggestion that they find a pair of skis and try it out. He preferred to lie on the deck and improve his suntan. Mel programmed the autopilot not to drift and joined Teld on the deck.

He watched her out of the corner of his eyes. " You might cause a navigation hazard with that costume," he said.

She unhooked the top and lay down. " In that case I won't wear it," she replied. " Besides, it's more fun sun-tanning like this. You don't get embarrassing white stripes and I get buzzed by handsome young pilots in copters."

She stretched out and closed her eyes. After a few moments hesitation he followed suit. " Did you bring the lotion ?" she asked.

" In the bag," he replied lazily, pulling it open and throwing her the bottle. She waited for a moment, then shrugged and rubbed the cream on with exaggerated vigour.

After she finished the bottle landed directly in Teld's midriff. He sat up, and unscrewed the top, then carefully leaned over her, trying not to block the sun from her eyes, and poured a generous helping of the cream between her breasts.

She raised herself on her elbows and glared at him. The yellow liquid ran sluggishly down her stomach, turned left at her hip and dripped heavily on to the deck.

" That," she said quietly, " was unfair."

" There's still some left," he replied, holding the bottle up and squinting at it.

" I'll pour it down your throat," she replied aggressively and snatched the bottle back, wiping the sticky fluid off with a towel and rubbed in some more. Then she lay back down and covered her eyes with lenses.

" Once I would have poured it down your throat," she amended.

" I like 'em with spirit," Teld said. " What changed your mind?"

" The fact that I'm getting old."

" Oh dear," he mocked.

" Too old for hanging round the Complex and running errands round the world for our masters in Brussels," she continued.

" What exactly do you do other than lure young scientists into Government contracts?" he inquired.

" Just that," she replied. " Call me a ' recruiting officer ' if you like. Also security . . . I suppose it's really more of a jack-of-all-trades when you tot up all the different aspects. Still, it's interesting or was. I don't like certain parts of it, though, such as investigating your background."

"You did what?" he shouted.

"Well, it was my job," she replied defensively. "Once we decided that Household had to go we looked around to see what could be salvaged from it, picked on you and went on from there."

"I suppose you followed me round as well," he said.

"I did not pry," she said stiffly. "What could be found out through easily accessible channels was naturally tried first. After all, you can't blame us, as prospective employers, from finding out what kind of person you were."

"I thought it would be too much to expect semi-privacy these days," he sighed.

"I only did what I thought necessary!" she flared.

"That's a load off my mind." He thought back. "I suppose you were on Arran with me?"

"No," she replied in a small voice. "I thought I'd give you a holiday."

He laughed. "Thank you very much."

Her slap caught him unawares, and his impulse to hit back was stopped through shock. They looked at one another for a moment, both tense, till Mel's shoulders slumped and she lay back down to look at the sky. "It's over now," she pleaded. "Leave it alone." He thought he could see a tear in the corner of her eye.

He went into the cabin and brought out a bottle of red wine, uncorked it, put the open top to his lips and drank several mouthfuls before passing it over to her.

After a second's hesitation she joined him, and they put the bottle just within reach before curling up into each other's arms.

" Nothing like the hair of the dog," he said. She could taste the wine in his breath, and far from revolting her, it seemed to relax her even more. Getting high on it, she decided ruefully.

" Except hangover pills, possibly," she replied. They both drank a little more, wiping their lips with the back of their hands afterwards and breaking out laughing at the sight. " You know you're not really that civilised yourself, Teld," she said when they'd recovered.

" It took four years of college to teach me these vices," he replied. " I'm not going to give them up that easily. And if you count civilised behaviour as being programmed to bow when a lady passes by and smile when the bugs bite, then I suppose I'm pretty uncivilised. Compared with the rest of the people in Central Europe. On the other hand, you don't look too civilised yourself lying there in a thin coating of cream."

" That's because I have my priorities right," she said. " I call my chief sir and carry on clandestine relationships with the staff. It's a form of compensation for my happy childhood. Everyone else I know was deprived and became extremely unstable and immature. You don't know how isolated that made me feel. Did you have a happy childhood?"

" All right, I suppose. My parents weren't too bad, but they weren't particularly brilliant at bringing up children, either. I hope I never make their mistakes."

" Which were?"

He dwelled on the answer for a moment. " I really couldn't pinpoint it," he replied. " It was a lot of different things. My father was a computer technician, my mother was a marine biologist. American, but you probably know that. Why I went Stateside to study. But I didn't see much of her. She died in the Challenger Deep disaster, and I don't think my father ever really adjusted to the situation." Her hand crept into his. " He married again, but I doubted whether he was happy."

" What happened?" she asked.

" They both died in a copter crash, along with a lot of other scientists."

" My father's still living," she said when he had got over his memory. " He'll be livid if he finds out I've shacked up with a younger man. He always had such high hopes for me, thought I might become a politician. Well, I'm in the Government now but he still doesn't like my job. Or my fellas."

" Who's your chief?" he asked.

" Someone who shall remain nameless in Brussels. I say that because he's also in charge of Holm which is probably why we dislike each other so much. I think he might be priming me to take his place."

" Would you?"

" No fear. I've got enough stashed away to say goodbye to Modular, the Complex and Sweden with disrespect. I can go and live in the South of France and you will be my consort. I have a yacht there, actually. Not very big, but she eats up berthing fees and needs two to run her."

" Never had much time for this," Teld admitted, waving the bottle around to indicate the sea. " Always too busy passing exams."

" Then enjoy it," she said.

" You won't be going for a while, will you?"

She shook her head and closed her eyes to sun.

* * *

Back in their hotel room she checked their clothes and possessions to find out whether they had been tampered with or searched. She found neither bugs nor bombs. Satisfied that they were both safe, she went out with Teld on a tour of the town. The craze for nostalgia had even hit Vortstag. They found two of the five restaurants were almost replicas of the one they had dined in at London. Morosely, Teld wondered how farther back the clock could retreat and considered setting up a costume hire business dealing exclusively in lionskins. He dropped it when Mel gave him a cost analysis of the project.

They returned to the hotel both tired and slightly drunk. The desk receptionist told Teld that a Dr. Fourneir had been trying to contact him since early evening. Teld promised to phone from his room and promptly forgot all about the matter. Back down in the lobby the girl tried to placate the doctor, who'd just rung through to discover that despite the fact Teld was in the building no one could reach him. Apparently the phone had been disconnected. In a fit of pique Fourneir rang off. The receptionist shrugged at the odd behaviour and switched on her earset, listening to the latest crisis bulletin with the same indifference she usually paid to the weather report.

* * *

The next day turned out to be even warmer than the previous one and the two lovers were showing signs of imminent suntans. They took the cruiser back to the same spot they'd found the day before and prepared to lie back and soak up the sun. The urgent call of the communicator brought Teld back to the cabin.

" Where the hell have you been," Fourneir demanded when Teld picked up the handset. " I've been trying to get in touch with you for the last twelve hours. Didn't the receptionist tell you I'd called?"

" I must have forgotten about it," Teld confessed. " I was rather far gone."

" So are things over here. Everyone's been rushing about like their tails are on fire." Fourneir quietened and became his usual self. " Things have cooled down for the moment, but there's no telling when we'll next hit a high point."

" What peaked this one?"

" Mobilisation of Africa. Apparently some of the American bases there have been put to full alert. Nobody's actually given any orders yet for the missiles to be readied but it can't be far off. We judge the next high will occur probably when the two sides meet for re-negotiation talks. How soon can you two get back?"

" Well . . . is it strictly necessary?"

" You know it is!"

Teld sighed. " All right. We're on our way." He turned to Mel. " Did you hear that?"

" Yes." She cancelled the autopilot and brought the cruiser round towards the shore. " I think it's lousy we should have to give up our holiday. Haven't you scientists any concern for others?"

" I'll phone Geneva and have them hold their jaw session till you've finished your suntanning."

" Don't talk about it," she said. " The subject bores me."

They arrived at the harbour and secured the boat, to the surprise of the owner, and collected their luggage from the hotel. The sun had just reached the zenith when Teld's aircar left the village and edged inland. Mel, in an uncharacteristic bad humour, said nothing. They had just lost sight of the coastal town when she glanced at the speedo and broke her silence. " You're speeding," she said, and looked up at the mirror. " You see? You've even got a police car following us. Slow down."

" All right," he said, and brought his foot off the accelerator. With thc braking action of the forward turboes the car came to a halt. Mel was still watching the mirror and when the other car came into view she jammed her foot down hard on the accelerator. The aircar leapt forward again and Teld found himself too occupied with steering to ask what had happened. Once he'd brought the car round to the road with Mel's foot still down hard on the pedal, he could afford to momentarily leave the road and look at the mirror. The car was still following them . . . but it wasn't any police car.

"Who the hell are they?" he asked.

"I don't know," Mel said, fumbling for her transceiver which had fallen between the seats. "Can you take the gas pedal for a moment?"

They changed over and while she tried to contact the Complex he followed the progress of the aircar behind them. It was steadily but surely catching up on them, and they were already at maximum speed. He quickly calculated that they'd never make the perimeter in time. "Just keep your eyes on the road," Mel hissed. "I'll keep a look out." He glanced down and saw in her lap, next to the transceiver, a small gas pistol. For a moment he couldn't think of anything else except the sleek black shape.

In order to gain a slight advantage over the other car Teld was keeping to the left of the road, where most of the curves turned. This had the negative aspect of bringing them closer to the roadside beacons. In his mind's eye Teld could see the charges piling up. But at least it would bring the police out to discover what was happening. Unfortunately, by then it might be too late.

"Bring us down," Mel said coldly. She held the gun stiffly in one hand, nervously twisting the dial on the broken transceiver with the other. He kept blindly on the road, praying that another vehicle wouldn't suddenly appear round a curve.

"I said bring us down," she repeated fiercely. No, he said to himself, and taking a firm grip on the wheel brought the car on to maximum lift and over the barrier into the open air.

The sharp change in direction took them both by surprise. Mel cannoned into Teld, who nearly lost his now precarious grip on the wheel. For an instant he had a giddy view of the ground twenty feet below to which he was rapidly dropping. There was only the howl of the vernier jets and the panoramic view to the front of the car to tell them they were still turning. Mel gave a half-stifled scream as the barrier suddenly appeared and passed just under them. They cleared it and bound upwards as the jets came into contact with the road surface.

The grey aircar was directly underneath them.

A few yards on Teld brought the car to an abrupt halt and cautiously approached the wreck of the grey aircar. It had tried to turn while under the full impact of the jets and had shot into the barrier like the proverbial seed from between two fingertips. The front was unrecognisable, almost welded as it was to the barrier. The rear of the vehicle stuck into the air but settled abruptly as the jets cut out. The steady deep-throated scream of the barrier klaxon hardly made any impression on their nerves. They stopped by the car and still with her pistol ready Mel looked over the wreck. When she returned she looked ill. " You'd better get us back," she said. " The police will be here in a minute." As they pulled away they could hear a new note enter the cacophony from that siren. That would be the police, Teld thought, and rounded the curve he had chosen for the turn.

" Do you think the police will come after us?" he asked her.

" No. With any luck they'll be more interested in the

crash than the barrier records and won't bother to look at them till they get back to the station. Then we can expect trouble. The Swedish police don't like cloak-and-dagger mysteries on their doorstep."

"Who do you think it was?"

"I don't know. I only wish there'd been more left of him to find out. Jesus, he was a mess. Where did you learn that?"

"Just now," he replied unhappily.

"Hmmph. Well, I'm only glad they decided to try and stop us while we were out here, and not in the town. We would have been rather pushed for elbow room . . . especially with your aerobatics."

A few miles further on the perimeter appeared and they halted at the gate while their passes were checked. Once inside the grounds, Mel said: "We'll have to see Holm about this, you know. Do you want to come with me or shall I see him myself? I know him of old and can deal with him."

"We'll both go," he said firmly.

Once they told him what had happened the old man was furious. "You should have waited for the police," he said. "You've both got diplomatic immunity. Now they'll be looking all over the countryside for you two and turn up here with a search warrant we can't possibly meet. I'll have to call them—why didn't you call me?" he asked Mel.

"My transceiver didn't work," she said, placing the broken instruments on the desk.

He looked at the transceiver for a moment, then

shrugged. " All right. You knew the dangers of being followed. He mightn't've, but you did, Mel."

" I know," she said resignedly. " It's our fault we were being tailed. Holm, it's puzzling me why you don't blame the International Communist Conspiracy on me."

" It's crossed my mind," he replied sourly. " Just as soon as I find enough evidence that will stand up in court you'll be there. Now get out, both of you. You've left me with enough work to get on with."

Outside the office Mel turned furiously to Teld. " Did you hear that?" she demanded shrilly.

Teld shrugged. " Don't expect me to be struck by all this undercover business. I'm new here, and I don't like being followed around—by anyone. I'm going to the Penthouse to see what's brewing. I'll meet you later."

" Don't get into any trouble," she warned.

* * *

By the time he reached the Penthouse only Fourneir and Michelson were left. Michelson stared fixedly out into the wallscreen while Fourneir was going through a thick roll of printout. " Where's everyone?" Teld asked, bewildered.

" They've gone home," Fourneir replied. " We're on shifts now. You and Rogov are here from twelve midnight to eight, Leighton's on from eight till four, Mitch and I take up the rest. You'd better go home and get some sleep."

" What's going on?" he demanded.

"I don't know," Fourneir said. "The computer must have spotted something we'd missed. The pattern probability it gives for war runs way over the high of this morning. There's something going on somewhere."

Teld glanced at the readout and shrugged. Fourneir was right. The pattern the computer showed was well in excess of a certainty. Yet there were no war rumbles. No one had launched anything. "Could the computer be jammed from outside?" he asked Fourneir.

"I doubt it," the scientist replied. "We've got all manner of fancy safeguards International assured us would work. If they've fallen down on the job we'd have known it before now. Like I said, go home and get some sleep. I'll call if there're any new developments."

He had barely entered the flat when the phone began to ring. He picked up the receiver. "Hello there," said Rogov. "I've just heard about your little escapade this afternoon."

"That was quick," Teld replied.

"We've got the most efficient grapevine in the business here," he went on. "You know we're on some sort of shift system."

"Fourneir just told me."

"It's beginning to bother me the way he pushes us around," Rogov continued. "And now after what happened to you I expect Holm'll put us all under martial law."

"So? Leon, I'm too tired at the moment to help you through your paranoid romances—"

The line clicked dead. He scowled and dialled Mel's

office number. "Do you always work Sunday afternoons?" he asked when she picked up her phone.

"Not when I'm needed elsewhere," she replied.

"You are. I'm clocking in at twelve tonight, and I don't think I should be disturbed before then. Looks like you'll have to move back to your own place for a while."

"Not even if I clock in with you?" she asked.

"You'd better hurry," Teld said.

"I've a few phone calls to make first," she said. "I want to get my story about what happened today to Brussels before Holm can stick his oar in."

"You'd better make it sound plausible," he said. "Don't forget I'm involved.

"Since you were driving I'm going to have to think very hard about how to shift the blame," she said. "But give me twenty minutes and I'll do it."

"It's a date, then," he said. After resetting the handset he wandered into the kitchen and made some thin soup from what he could find lying around in the freezer. It helped to pass the time, even if the results were inedible.

CHAPTER SIX

THE FLOUROS in the Penthouse had been burning continuously for eight hours and one had developed a persistent buzz that set Teld's teeth on edge. Rogov had phoned maintenance to complain about it but in the two hours since no one had arrived to replace it.

Teld's mouth was bitter from drinking too much coffee and his eyes were aching from strain. Sometimes he had to forcibly focus them in order to make out the characters on the display screens. He felt hot and dry in his clothes and wished for the hundredth time someone had thought of including a shower in the design of the Penthouse.

Rogov was in front of one of the terminals, reading the information as it was passed along. In Geneva the politicians were still talking behind closed doors and there was no sign whatsoever of either side backing down from the full alert all military bases were on. Europe had alerted her own some time ago, and every single terminal with access to the computer must have been in use. If they hadn't switched to exclusive display screen readout the two scientists would have been knee deep in line print. He interrupted his vigil to sweat at the irritating noise of the flouro and phoned maintenance again. " They say they can't get anyone out this late at night," he called over to Teld, without bothering to cover the mike with his hand.

" Then tell them we'll do it ourselves if they can send us the flouro," Teld replied. The chemical which glowed brightly in the presence of an electromagnetic field seemed to have dimmed slightly, casting a grey shadow on whoever walked under it. Rogov seemed to argue with whoever was on the other end of the line, then slammed the phone down.

" I think we ought to call Fourneir," Rogov said. " DaSilva's condition is worsening."

" You think it's poisoning?" Teld asked.

" It's a very inconvenient heart attack otherwise," Rogov pointed out.

" Surely the Americans don't think the Russians had anything to do with it," Teld asked.

" Whether they think that or not the damned pattern's gone up again," Rogov replied.

" I'll call him," Teld said, and phoned his home direct. Ginita answered, and promised to fetch Dave immediately.

" Fourneir here," he said at last. " What's up?"

" DaSilva's been taken up with a heart attack and it now looks as though it was engineered," Teld replied.

" What's his condition?"

" Critical. The doctors don't hold out much hope. The

pattern's up to ninety-two. Another three and we'll have to order the orbiting platforms . . ."

" I know, I know," Fourneir said. " I'll be over right away. Have you rung Mitch or Leighton ?"

" No. Should I ?"

" Better not. They'll hear the sirens. If it comes to that. What's the President doing ?"

" We don't know. He's still in conference. He knows about DaSilva but he hasn't made any statements yet."

Over the telephone Fourneir sounded very tired. " Keep an eye on things," he said. " I'll be right over.

* * *

The night had carried its share of violence. Mel had long since tired of listening to reports of demos and riots which had turned into orgies of destruction when the police had converged on them. She switched channels on the teli and heard that the American Secretary of State had suffered a heart attack and was lying in a Swiss hospital Monitor tank. Someone suspected poisoning and he had undergone a blood transfusion. Tomorrow's papers would carry the news . . . if there was going to be a tomorrow.

She slipped out of her bed and dressed in casual jeans and blouse, then poured herself a glass of milk. Carrying some fruit and the glass she returned to the bedroom and assembled the picnic on the bed, sitting cross-legged in front of the teli and gnawing at an apple. Oddly enough she didn't feel as tired as she normally would this time in the morning. There must be something about crises, she thought. The newstapes were going over the same old material again and again and again. In frustration she switched off. Why weren't they telling her what she wanted to know, she asked herself angrily.

After a while she lay back and with her naked foot polarised the mirror over her bed. The glass plate seemed to haze as the chemical backing darkened and in a few seconds she looked up at herself. Her hair was splayed back over the pillow, tangled and slightly dry. She looked —and felt—old. Her eyes were veined with a fine red web-pattern. Her body was relaxed, but not in the attitude of compromised femininity she allowed herself with Teld, but the manner of a weariness which was too deep and familiar to be felt any more. How I've let myself get this way, she thought. Why did it happen to me?

The mirror didn't reply. She brought her hands up to touch her face and slight lines which she had only just noticed. Growing old, she continued. And I thought the yoga would help me.

In sudden decision she turned the mirror off and left the bedroom, only stopping on the way to her office for a pair of shoes. Outside, in the corridor, no one noticed her as she rushed by. She guiltily realised that she hadn't bothered to put a support on, and her breasts felt as though they were flopping all over the place. Well, let 'em, she decided. The exercise might do them some good. She punched the floor number into the lift and ordered an override over intermediate floor stops. There'd be a few startled faces among those who'd waited for the lift.

Her office was quiet—almost dead, she thought, and she carried the electric typewriter from her secretary's desk into her own office and swept the papers, pen holders and objects off the worktop with one fluid motion of her arm. Then she sat down and inserted a sheet of paper into the carriage and thought. Eventually she gave up and just pressed her finger down on the x key and left it there. The carriage sped across the body, with the key dancing back and forth in a manic rhythm, till the letters divided the paper in two. She still kept her finger on the key, and the platen clicked two spaces up and zipped back to start the whole operation all over again.

As soon as the exercise bored her she took her fingertip away and left the machine to hum over to itself. She crossed to the window and looked out into the night, switching off the flouros so she could improve her night vision. After a few seconds she could make out details; there were more guards than ever out on patrol and the aircars never went anywhere unless in pairs. That, she thought, was banal. Two aircars wouldn't stop a missile. And none of the people were likely to riot here in the Complex. If war-crazed Swedes from the surrounding countryside decided to invade the place . . . she smiled at the thought. But that wasn't important. She was important, and so was Teld. They owed nothing to anyone other than themselves. That was the basis of life, wasn't it? Of survival, then. She could go whenever she liked—Teld knew and appreciated that. He could follow if he liked, though she knew he would and to decide arbitrarily would not be fair to him. But what would they do? Just lie around all day? Neither of them would be happy doing that.

There was a knock on the door. She looked up, puzzled, and tried to think who knew she was there. She remembered leaving the outer office door open when she came in. Better see who it is and send him away, she decided, opening her office door.

A guard was standing in the office, looking around. "What is it?" she demanded.

"Just checking, ma'am," the guard replied. "Orders from Colonel Holm."

"Well, you'd better go back and report to him that you are getting under the feet and skin of this civilian. Now go away. I've got work to do."

The man coloured but he merely saluted wordlessly and left. She shut the door and after a moment's thought, locked it.

* * *

Fourneir arrived in the Penthouse at two forty-three and threw his briefcase on to the top of the table, scratching the veneer. Two surly technics were working at the flouro. The A class handyman who usually attended to such jobs was on holiday. Once they'd left, Fourneir lit a cigarette and slumped into a chair. "What's the latest?" he asked.

"No change in DaSilva's condition," Teld replied, tonelessly. "The Soviets deny any connection with the incidence and the doctors have definitely ascertained that he was poisoned. It must have happened at the reception dinner a few hours ago. The rest of Europe's pretty bad. Rioting everywhere, protesting about the two superpowers being allowed to fight things out over a conference table here when we're not even neutral territory. Even this late at night. The authorities have cancelled all rapitrans services due to vandalism in stations and what that's doing to the transport situation is terrifying."

" Well, looks like things have finally reached the boiling point," Fourneir diagnosed. " You'd better put the launch programmes into the computer giving the missiles their targets." He opened the suitcase and handed over a set of wafer-thin cassettes, each with their own acceptance code. Teld and Rogov fed them into the input channel. The final commitment, Teld thought. He finished and moved back to look at the wildly flashing display screens.

Fourneir stubbed out his cigarette. " When I was young I can remember going on nuclear disarmament marches to Aldermaston in protest against the stockpiling of weapons. Didn't do much good, though, neither did the SALT talks, either, but it showed the world that the young people wouldn't sanction world blackmail or war the way the older generation had thirty years before. Mind you, war was fresher in our minds then than it is to the same set of people now." He smiled at the memories. " In those days we used to have a very good excuse for premarital sex, as it was called then. If anyone asked why we couldn't wait a few years until we were old enough to marry we'd tell them we doubted very much if there was going to be a tomorrow. The last disarmament march we made, years after the disbanding of the Civil Defence, was in nineteen seventy-seven. Since then nothing, except for the occasional news reports about stockpiling or the testing of another safe bomb. Perhaps we ought to have a small war every ten years just to show people how terrible armed conflict really is and why they should continue to protest about it. The worst time came in sixty three, when the Russians were discovered building missile bases on Cuba, a small island off the American coast, itself politically communist—"

"The Bay of Pigs episode," Rogov said knowledgeably. "We were told about it."

"That's what I'm trying to point out to you," said Fourneir, lighting another cigarette. "You haven't experienced it, they read about it in what they're too ashamed to call History any more, but grace it with such names as Social Studies or whatever. By the same token you could present Philosophy as psychology nowadays. Anyway—the two world leaders then were Kennedy and Krushchev. Kennedy was assassinated not long afterwards, the man who brought the world back from the brink of nuclear disaster. JFK threatened the Russians with war if they didn't withdraw from Cuba. Eventually the Russians dismantled their missiles and shipped them back to the Continent, leaving the Balance of Prudence, or to be more correct, Terror in place. When the first pix of missile carriers appeared in the papers I thought, "Well, that's that" and persuaded some girl to come camping with me in North Wales. It was three weeks to the day when we returned to civilisation—"

On the display screen, in an almost religious presentation of black and white appeared the words:

DaSilva dies in Swiss hospital 03:01 am (Reuter)

Fourneir appropriately enough, ignored it. "—and discovered that several days before the Russians had backed down. Actually, we'd been more interested in ourselves than the survival of civilisation. I met her again three years later, and we settled down till cancer killed her."

"Didn't you have radiacs then?" Rogov asked.

"Not to the extent we can use dissolved isotopes now. Then they irradiated the whole area over the tumour, admittedly killing off a lot of cancer cells but also poisoning a lot of others as well. When they developed DMSO we could treat the tumours direct, but then I'm talking about a medical science which had only just come into qualifying as a science. It was very fashionable for cancer scares those days, what with cigarettes—"

The phone rang. He picked it up and listened for a moment before shouting, "Look, I can't take time out to give you status reports, Holm, and my colleagues are far too busy to be pestered by you. This line should be kept open, so get off it this bloody minute. If you can't borrow a radio to listen to find yourself a clairvoyant." He gave the others a half-smile. "That man gets on my bloody goat. Thing is, we need that line open. Our leaders will be demanding advice, and a few of those men in business suits will be wondering how fast they make the shelters. In this type of situation, there're only two times: too early, and too late."

He sat down to wait, not looking tired at all, but just fazed and bright-eyed. "Had anything to eat yet?" he asked. "I'll call for some sandwiches and coffee. How's the pattern running now?"

"Not high enough to initiate launch sequences," Teld reported. "Just enough to make us sweat, though."

"Better warn Mitch and Leighton about the situation, tell them not to start out here, this thing might grab them right in the middle. Use the other phone. And call anyone you might hold dear to yourself. I know it's favouritism but that's the way I feel. Rog, you too."

The phone by his elbow rang again. He picked it up. "Brussels?" he asked. "Where the hell have you been? Put me through and don't hang about. Hello. Alessandro? Nice to hear from you, too. You want to know what our wonderful computer's doing? Arming your nuclear warheads, that's what. Now they've just been primed. Yes, it's that serious. No, don't run for the hills yet, Alessandro, I want to talk with you."

Teld smiled to himself and ordered reception to page Mitch and Leighton. After relaying Fourneir's instructions, he tried Mel's apartment, then his own, and finally her office. After the third ring the phone was answered. She sounded dull.

"That you?" he asked.

"Yes," she replied. "How much time have we got?"

" Plenty, more than enough if we don't panic. Go back to the apartment, and start to pack some clothes into an overnight bag, and don't forget some sedatives from the bathroom cupboard. There probably won't be enough in the shelter. Dump that next to the door and stay there."

" Yah sur," she replied.

" And don't be impertinent."

" Yes, sir," she corrected.

" That's better. Now off you go. See you later—"

" —moderator," she completed. He put down the phone and Rogov took his place. Three twenty-two and the President had left the meeting chambers. He looked at the display screens. At least things were holding.

* * *

Although she had already prepared an emergency kit, she rechecked it over and added a couple of packets of Long Night sleeping tabs, then lit an Acapulco Gold and after a moment's thought, took two from the packet and slipped the rest into the overnight bag. Then she went to the bedroom, switched on the teli, and sat drawing heavily on the exquisitely made joint and listening to the commentator's words. He was describing the riot which occurred in a subway station outside Lyons. Over five hundred people had been involved when a rapitrans express came through the station, having been redirected by the routing officer, who later committed suicide. Over a fifth were killed by the sudden vacuum effect as the express passed through, smashing themselves against the sides of the carriages, but the rest were equally doomed. The explosive decompression which resulted from the rapitrans leaving the station taking most of the atmosphere underground with it. Doors had been blown inwards by the drop in pressure and a gory newstape showing the messy walls of the subway made her feel ill. Belatedly, she realised she should never have lit the joint, or for that matter watched the news. She would never hit nirvana the way she was feeling. But it was too late now and an adolescence spent cherishing every last millimetre prevented her from stubbing it out. For some time it lay hanging in her fingers, the sweet aromatic smell hanging in the air till the ash tumbled down on to her jeans. Brushing it off, the ash was sent into the air to make crazy patterns before settling on to the carpet, where she ground it in with her foot.

She decided that she would have to take some momentoes of the years gone by before they were destroyed. In her bedside cupboard was fifteen years' worth of history, a few precious stereographs, thick crystalline cubes which images burnt into the molecular ' memory ' which passed light through that *angle* and then out *there* producing the illusion of an image. Wrapping them in cotton she also slipped those in the bags. Sitting back she took a last drag and then crumbled the butt into the ashtray. Roaches, she thought, that's what they used to be called in the old days on the streets. In her mind's eye she could recall the blue-and-red licences now, with the photostat signature of the police chief and the solid computer type on the pages. Where had all those things gone, she wondered briefly. Her den, for when she hadn't been travelling alone. Hocked, if she could remember correctly, when her partner had been picked up in Germany. Ach, those days hadn't been so civilised then. Not with a new totalitarian type government just in power and the first of the Peace casualties coming in.

There would be no harm, she decided, in a little music. A cartridge slipped into the record player supplied that commodity. It was, funnily enough, Metamorphosis, by Richard Strauss. Not that she had much time to pick favourites nowadays, but it was the tune she remembered most often. Concertos and symphonies and that stuff flew out of her head in no time: the weirdness that was the Metamorphosis stayed.

It was hard to believe that in just a couple of years—supposing they survived them—the new century would arrive. The opening bars of the recording stirred her inner chord (somewhere she'd punned that) and she wanted very much to survive those years. The human race had built so much these past thousands of years, too much to be thrown away overnight. The tragedy would be so great as to be meaningless. How could you explain away the radioactive stumps of great civilisations left behind for future historians?

Furiously she punched the rewind button, hoping to catch again a melody she might never hear again. Even if things did not fall apart, they would never recover from the war, or even from the threat of war. The question of Europe's future was no longer important. They would never be free, whatever the politicians said, so long as the missile silos and the technicians waiting calmly behind their flight computers searched the skies for the first trace of invading MIRVs existed. If the world did survive, the bases would not. They carried within them the seeds of their own destruction, if not the rest of the world's. Still, there was a yacht moored at Matigues. Vaguely, she wondered how long it would take them to cross Europe, supposing that Europe was still habitable. Or a hundred things didn't happen to them on the way—they could try.

* * *

" The patterns place strike time at somewhere round six this morning," said Rogov.

" I'm not going to argue with the computer," said Fourneir. " And it's four hundred now. We can run the launch sequence just as effectively from the shelter." The sandwiches arrived. " You realise that we're far better off than anyone else in the world right now, of course."

" And how do you make that out?" Teld asked.

" We're in a non-strike area. We've a whole battery of missile-laden subs round the coast ready to intercept anything heading this way, and a computer like this to direct operations, not forgetting the shelter—how can we lose out? These sandwiches are really very good, you know. If this is what the canteen can turn out under stress then we ought to run Armageddon every lunchtime."

The communicator on the conference table buzzed for attention. Fourneir ignored it. " If the strike is set for six this morning we'll get the tracking stations notified. We've some innocent-looking radio-telescopes secretly hooked to the computer—and why not? The more fixes it has the better its aim. Still no launch signal from Big Bear, though."

Michelson had been listening in on the communicator, switched on while Fourneir had been talking to Leon. "I agree with what you say. The orbiting platforms will be the last resort of the aggressors. They're far too open and vulnerable to attack. It'll be the bases we don't know about which'll launch the first missiles, intended to soften up opposition, before the other silos are hit, then if there's no armistice forthcoming, they'll use the rest of what they've got."

Teld began to fidget, Fourneir waved Rogov to silence. The waiting was beginning to erode his patience. He wondered what Mel was doing.

"We've got military advisors to tell us who's going to hit first, where, when and with what," Fourneir said. "But they forget to give some to tell us what to do while we wait. We're in the hands of people who play war-games for a living, and up till now the question of war has been academic, but now it's a matter of when rather than if, and that when might be just ninety-eight minutes away. With luck, we'll come through without any real scratches. Just a few badly messed up pieces of real estate here and there. If things fall the other way—then we won't know anything about it anyway, and I for one will be most grateful. But till that time, we don't panic, and we don't argument. No argument over 'we can't do it—you're wrong ' and we may find out that our survival, and not the war, is academic, perhaps fixed. Is that understood?"

Reluctantly, the other two nodded. " All right," Fourneir said, " let's not collapse into a pile of nervously twitching line and see what there is left we can do."

* * *

By now she had reached the window and stood looking out into the night, waiting for the brief but spectacular nuclear dawn. She felt sleepy, very tired and knew that if she went to sleep now it would be very likely that she would never wake up again, so she wanted to stay awake and watch the dawn a last time. The high from the joint had left her—they were never so strong as they were in the old days, the street days, you could really get stoned then. She had more of a grip on herself, though. In the bathroom she had tried to freshen herself with a splash of cold water. A moment later, the tiredness returned. She sighed and in the lounge tested the weight of the bag. Far too heavy and she hardly remembered putting the souvenirs inside. The joints, though, remained. If they ran out of Long Nights they could use them instead, or barter them for other stuff. Just in case anyone decided to search their bag intending to steal anything valuable she hid the packets down the sleeve of a jumper, where they couldn't be felt. She replaced the stereos on the bedside cupboard. In the shelter they would have what they stood up in and a change of clothes, plus some drugs of both descriptions. She had called Cleo and told her to assemble a similar package, but the young girl had objected to the thought of having the drugs along. The Neopuritan upbringing of some of the more modern kids quite frankly amazed her. The prophets of her youth had proclaimed that the age of repression was over and that no one would have to suffer from the cultural conditioning of society again.

Well, they'd been wrong in this, just as in all the other predictions they'd made and now, with the light of today thrown on their words, they were just as senselessly arrogant. The broad-minded teenager is often the hermetically-sealed intellect of middle age. Now if she ever had to bring up children (Teld's?) she knew how she would go about it. But there again, what right had she for thinking that? Despite what she may say about herself, she was still young, rich if cynical. And waiting for a bomb to fall, somewhere.

There would not be much she'd miss losing in the event of war, she decided, if Teld stayed with her. That itself proved something, she wasn't so cynical as to think that all love was beyond her. Smugly happy in the thought that at least she hadn't got herself prematurely hitched to anyone, she was left to pick and choose (even if the final choice was his) and everything had worked out fine. She could at least see a little daylight ahead for them. What'll it be like, she wondered, if we had to build everything up again? Just those few left alive? Could they go back to an awareness of innocence, with the crawling city monsters eradicated from the globe? Or would it be an existence of moving from one shell to another, in cities depopulated by bombs? What would they do in a world like that, go where?

* * *

"Brussels want to know how long they've got," Fourneir said after he'd put the phone down. "I told them they'd be linked directly with attack procedure through the computer. It's their choice whether they stay above ground and watch the show or go underground. I should think they'd be at least a first generation secondary target for someone."

"But that's their problem. I'll bet there're people biting their nails and covering their ears in the Kremlin and the White House. No reason why we should think ourselves any more radiation-proof. You'd better advise Holm we're opening up the shelters, Leon."

Teld wiped away a lot of the perspiration on his forehead, and discovered that his hair was sticky and damp. "Are you going to sound the sirens?" he asked.

"No sense in worrying anyone, is there?" Fourneir said.

"Holm says to leave the shelters shut. He's afraid someone'll run in, close the doors behind them and leave the rest of us to fry," Rogov said.

"There's not much he can do about that," Fourneir said, tripping a switch. "They're open now." He stubbed his cigarette out and listened to the clamour of alarm bells. "He seems to be capitalising on the fact. Well, until the attack sirens sound he'd better stay where he is with the rest of his pestilential troops."

"There it goes," said Teld, solemnly, looking into the display screen. Over the alarms they could hear the strident tone of the attack sirens, a throbbing ululation which in time drowned everything else.

CHAPTER SEVEN

FOURNEIR LISTENED to the alarms a moment longer, then held up his hands. " All right. You know where to go. I'll go on to the Village shelter, while you two make for the one in the Block. When you get there, don't stop to kiss your girlfriends hello, just get into the computer room and tie it into our net." He studied the clock for a moment. " If everything's going to plan you have twenty-nine minutes to move about five hundred yards, so I don't want to hear about broken limbs. Good luck and see you later." He collected his empty briefcase and left the Penthouse. Teld and Rogov looked at each other, and then followed him after closing down the systems in the Penthouse.

They continued in the lift up to the top floors, disregarding the urgent commands of people waiting for the lift to take them down. Five floors from the top, Teld left the cage and walked down the corridor to his flat

Most of the doors were open, with the lights still left on in the rooms. He reached his door, and pressed on the platelock. The door slid open and he walked in. Mel was standing by the window, her hands palm down on the glass, looking out across the Complex to some hidden point. Her eyes were glazed and unfocused, and the heavy scent of hash was in the room.

"Are you coming or not?" he asked, picking up the overnight bag and pulling her round.

She came out of the trance slowly. "I missed them," she said. "Jesus, I'm tired."

"Missed what?" he asked.

"Nothing. No, something I was thinking about." She shook her head and leaned on him. "Sorry. I shouldn't have smoked."

"Doesn't matter. We're going to have enough trouble getting you down those steps without you tripping everyone with your breath. Here, have one of these." He gave her a couple of mints.

"Silly boy," she giggled, but chewed them all the same.

Outside the flat all was bedlam. They forced their way to the stairs but had to stand around while others blocked the lift entrance. Mel was grinning at everyone and could prove a possible menace if she wasn't sobered up soon enough, but in her state a brisk walk wouldn't have brought her down. They managed to reach the stairs and began to walk down a few levels to where guards were supervising the evacuation. One of them walked over and heaved Teld to one side. Before Teld had recovered his balance he was looking at Mel with a puzzled frown, while she beamed back at him. He didn't recognise her—no one would with that stupid smirk across her face, and the casual clothes, not forgetting her bra-less condition and—Christ, she's lost her sandals somewhere. He pulled the guard back and shouted something in his face. The guard stiffened, and Teld pushed him into the crowd. Then he ran his hands through his pockets, trying to find his security cards.

They were in a riot situation, he knew that much. If he didn't get Mel out of here fast she'd be crushed under the weight of bodies moving, perhaps hit, and certainly hurt. So, come to think of it, would he. The cards were in his back trouser pocket. He slipped them out, covering his with Mel's, so that her EXECUTIVE emblem was visible while his lack of it wasn't. The guard walked over to see what the trouble was and waved him through, glancing at the overnight bag but not sufficiently interested to look inside it.

Just as they reached the door he heard a scream and a thick slapping sound. Mel tried to turn and look but he pulled her back and down the stairs.

In a few minutes they were out into the night, unusually cold and active. Aircars were rushing about, disregarding the rule about only using the covered and reserved road-space. One dashed in front of them to be followed by several more. They'd wasted over twenty minutes in the Block. Where was the shelter?

Mel was in no condition to give a sensible reply. It was gradually sinking into her stoned mind that she was in a bad place and the tears were beginning to form in her eyes. Teld groaned and rocked back on his heels, trying to think. He orientated himself and started off towards the gaggle of people standing round the shelter entrance. There was a guard there, too. This was developing into a farce. Fortunately this one did recognise Mel and made a way for them both.

In the computer room he met Rogov. " Took your time," he said, looking up from a pamphlet. " You might as well sit yourself down and have some coffee."

" What's going on?" Teld asked. " I've never seen a panic like that on. They'll never get two hundred in here before the shelters close."

" I've overridden the original signal," Rogov replied. " Fourneir didn't like it, but he was faced with the same problem. You'll probably be glad to know someone broke Michelson's jaw. I'd rather it'd been Holm's, but Mitch would have been my second choice anyway."

" When you closing the doors?"

" When everyone's in," Rogov replied. " I'm not going to leave my friends out there just because that fascist Holm says they should have been here ten minutes ago. Hell, you've seen what it's like out there. Besides, we can't track the missile any more. It either came down in the sea or was meant for some other target. In any case, the heat's off." He threw the pamphlet on the floor and left the Computer room, came back a few seconds later and shut the doors. " That's it, everyone's in. Right. Now the whole world can go up as far as I'm concerned."

Mel appeared in the doorway, shielding her eyes against the harsh illumination and the glare from the tapedecks, printout units and terminals. " Thought you were going to sleep through it all?" Teld asked her gently.

" I want to," she said. " But I can't."

" Visitors welcome," said Rogov, and tactfully moved out of range.

" Anything being tracked?" he demanded, still holding Mel.

" Three MIRV traces, whose, I can't say. Point of origin, north coast of Africa. I don't know where they're going but it looks like Central Europe."

" Are you sure they're MIRVs?" Teld asked.

" Well, they're certainly big enough, but they could be those old un-safe bombs nobody's supposed to have and no one's supposed to know about."

" In that case their computing machinery'll be so ancient they couldn't evade anything we've got down there," Teld said. He looked over Rogov's shoulder at the radar screen and shuddered: the whole sky was criss-crossed with missile trails, both predicted and known.

Another screen was showing estimated bombing schedules—appointments with der Tag, he thought. Still, there was nothing he could do about altering them. From now on it would be a matter of waiting till the War was over, then finding out what areas had been hit.

" We should really celebrate with champagne this moment," Rogov said moodily. " What human civilisation has been working towards these past uncountable years. Self destruction."

" That hasn't been all," Teld reminded him.

" It's all that counts," Rogov pointed out. " Look at it —don't tell me that can't be one of the most beautiful sights in the Universe. What the earth will look like from space in half an hour—"

"You might get your wish if the platform crews haven't been knocked out," Teld replied. Apart from the radar there were satellites in orbit broadcasting information primarily intended for weather forecasts but which had been designed with another use in mind. There were two mercator projections of the world on the console, one which showed the world as green land, blue sea, and the other with small ringed red spots on the land which were known missile bases. Other screens were just for vision; one showed the North East Pacific, with the tip of California showing up to the San Joquin valley. He frequently turned to look at the missile traces, which were growing more numerous all the time. The nearest strike-time was just eight minutes away.

Abruptly the radio came to life. A drone of what sounded like Latin and static filled the Computer room. Rogov listened for a few moments, then shook his head and tried other frequencies. On the radar several of the traces entered Russian and American radar cover and a few were quickly and efficiently intercepted. A number, though, continued on their way inland.

As they approached their targets their courses changed, hopefully foxing serious pursuit into trying to determine their new paths. Not long afterwards the first bombs found their targets and the screen became very cloudy indeed.

* * *

The cubicle was even smaller than she had imagined it would be. There didn't seem to be any room at all for finding a comfortable sleeping position and in her hypercritical state of mind this was the most important purpose of the cubicle; sleep and not survival. By the time she was awoken, the high had worn off and she could look at things objectively again.

Teld was standing in the cubicle. There were rings under his eyes and he moved slowly and carefully, as though drunk. She checked the time, and found it far advanced into the afternoon. Assuming, of course, that she hadn't slept twelve hours plus whatever value she *had* slept—

" Is it over ?" she asked.

After a few moments he nodded and sat down on the edge of the narrow bed. " It's over all right. Most of North America is out, Russia has been badly hit, and so have China and India. There's been a strike in Central Europe somewhere."

" Then what's the position ?" she asked, attentive.

" All in all, we're still here. Should receive the first weather effects in a couple of days. Otherwise we're safe."

" Are you going back to the Computer room ?" she asked.

" Fourneir told us to get some sleep," he replied. " We won't be allowed out till after they're sure that all the war is over."

" Do you think it is ?"

" As far as I'm concerned, everything that's going to fall has fallen."

"What about the radio? Could you pick up anything?"

"God, you won't be able to hear anything for a while. The Van Allen belts'll be unsettled for days. Besides, anyone with a radio will want to conserve power for other things and'll wait until the dust settles."

She pulled a satchel from under the bed. "I found this. They call it a survival kit. There are some concentrates, if you want something to eat."

"Thanks," he replied, and pulled a cube off the slab she gave, him, carefully rewrapping the polythene cover. It tasted sweet and very dry. He swallowed a few mouthfuls of water from the carafe she gave him, and finished off the rest of the nougaty cube with a forced smile.

"There're some sedatives," she said, indicating the crumpled foil sachet. He dutifully swallowed one and stretched out on the space she left for him. He felt her move and after a few seconds the light of the corridor erupted into the cubicle, and just as quickly darkened. He turned to face the wall and slipped into a distinctly uneasy sleep.

* * *

The two hundred and twenty-four people who were housed in the shelter had fared well. No one had gone under the mental strain which pulled at them all, and everyone who was still awake seemed well behaved if a little apathetic and confused. A few were hungry and had opened their survival kit concentrates, which Mel wished they hadn't done, since there was a well-stocked kitchen in the shelter they could use for two months—which they might have to do. She would have preferred that the concentrates be kept against the time when their other supplies ran out. However, the concentrate was quite flexible in its way. The little handbook which came with the kit said you could eat it raw, make a soup from it, with a different thickness until it became a gravy, or—a category she added herself—could be thrown away. It still tasted much the same whatever you did to it.

Mel rose to the challenge of leading the shelter with characteristic enthusiasm. Her brisk business manner disposed of feminine opposition and her looks quelled male rebellion. The first problem was to organise meals, which she did on a purely rota basis, making sure that neither Teld, Rogov nor herself were included in it. By the time the first meal rolled round, she had turned one of the cubicles into an office and assumed complete command, pointing out that the more official her self-assumed role, the more authority she would carry. The only trouble with this attitude was that people began to look forward to a long stay in the shelter, which Teld thought totally wrong. "Look at it this way," Mel told him. "If they think that they're going to stay down here a long time they won't object to minor discomforts which are bound to make themselves felt even after only a few hours. On the other hand, if you informed them they were going to be out in just thirty-six hours, they'd be so taken up in counting downwards that after a while they'll be manic with impatience, demanding that they be let out *now*. If on the other hand, you can do any better—"

"Perhaps we ought to hold elections," he suggested.

"Certainly not! In an enclosed space like this we'd be at each other's throats in days. Things stay as they are."

Communication between the two main shelters by radio-phone was often hampered by the fierce electrical disturbance of the upper atmosphere which quite often blanketed out satellite signals as well, which Teld felt to be a pity, since the aurora produced by the after effects of the bombs would be extremely spectacular. They were lucky enough to catch one on an orbiting monitor, but the range was too great to be able to say whether much activity was going on or whether it was just a short-lived ion storm from the sun. Rogov discovered that this was the year for sunspots. Even so, the beautifully flickering majesty of the aurora evaded them time and time again. When communication was open with the platform crew they promised to transmit some film they'd made of the phenomena with a hand-held cine camera, just as soon as their own scientific crew got tired of playing it. The platform crew were in high spirits—they'd need to be, knowing that it might be many years before a ship could be built to ferry them back down from their ellipsoid path round the earth, and that their tour had originally been intended for just a few months. There was the chance that the Russian manned lunar expedition on Farside might help, but no one had heard anything from them since the war.

The platform had two command modules which could

return to earth under their own jets—but they were designed for splashdown in the Atlantic, with naval support close at hand. This wouldn't have been too difficult to arrange with the hundreds of seacraft still floating around the world—a submarine would have done in a pinch—but so far no contact had been made with any ships. Teld couldn't understand this, since the opportunity for radio contact was always taken when the atmospheric was clear enough, and could only hypothesise that the commanders of the ships had deliberately been ordered not to answer any signals as such until their centres of operation could tell them whether or not they were safe to make reply. And if the C.O.O. had been blown to neutrons in the war . . .

The first sign of trouble came on the second day in the shelter when they were theoretically only fifteen hours from release. Fourneir made a routine call, and after swapping chatter told Rogov to clear everyone except the two scientists from the Computer Room.

"We're the only ones here," Leon replied with a smile. "Nobody comes to visit us now Mel's taken over."

"That figures," Fourneir said. "The truth is, we've had a little trouble with our life support system. How's yours functioning?"

"Just checked it," Rogov replied. "Everything reads green. What's wrong with yours?"

"Well," Fourneir said with great reluctance, "our water filtration unit's packed up. Not only that but the pumps have come to a halt, as well. Some sections were flooded, others are bone dry. I think the trouble came when recycled water was used to bring the water level in the main tank back up to normal. Mind you, there's a hell of a strain on our system, we've close to a thousand people here, so yours might never crack up, but I thought it better to warn you."

"We'll keep tabs on it," Teld promised. "Anything else?"

"Not at the moment. If this radio noise keeps up, looks like we might have to stay in longer than we'd planned. Is there anything on your set?"

"No," Teld admitted. "Apart from a few chats with the platform crew, and only when the air's clear. How long do you reckon the interference will keep up?"

"Hard to say with the flares on the sun's surface, but they seem to be especially violent this year. Just our luck. Well, keep in touch—every three hours, if possible. I'll have some more information for you then, I hope."

Rogov turned the radio off and shook his head, "It's quiet out there. You get the carrier wave, but nothing else."

"No one should be broadcasting this early," said Teld. "Let's see what's—"

The rapid bleating of an alarm interrupted him. He looked over the display board, found the meter which had been causing the trouble. "Will you look at this," he said. "The recycling system's flooded."

"How?" Rogov demanded.

"I don't know. I'll have to go and examine the system. Not that I want to, but this could lead to flooding, and an electrical short is the last thing we want." He stood in thought for a moment. "The pumps could have reversed themselves," he added. "Don't know how, but that would explain—damn, I'll go and see myself. Hang on."

Wishing that he had brought swimming trunks with him he found a schematic of the shelter and traced the water ducts with his fingertip, mentally placing them in the shelter. After a while he felt as though he could find without too much difficulty the pumps that might be responsible. He opened the maintenance corridor and walked through, sealing it behind him and edging forward till the symbols in front of his eyes told him he had reached the pumps assembly. Bringing the inspection plate down he peered into the darkness, and discovered a small switch which turned on a battery operated light over the assembly. He gave the pumps a look over, couldn't find any leaks or worn insulation on the power leads, then turned the isolation key and began to unscrew the collar over one of the pipes joining the pump. When the collar suddenly slipped out of his hands and the pump whipped by his face, splashing it with cold water, he jerked his head back, narrowly missing a direct hit with the corridor wall.

Water was pouring out of the pipe and into the corridor. He tried to reach the pump with his hand but it had swung too far for him to reach. If he could only block the pipe, he thought, but lacked the necessary material for a stop. By now the water was on full force and he was in water up to his ankles. He had an uncomfortable idea of what thirty thousand gallons would do to the electrical systems, and to him in particular if he was trapped here.

He decided to make for the computer room and try and decide what to do there.

He never made it. A few feet from the seal the lights went out with a loud click and the corridor was thrown into darkness, with the only sound the steady gushing of water. Teld found the door and punched the open stud furiously. Nothing happened. By now the water was around his knees and he had to wade back to the only source of illumination, the battery inspection light. He could imagine what had happened. Rather than short the whole shelter, some safeguard had been tripped by the flooding and turned off the whole system. And the seal was operated by an electric lock. He kicked the wall savagely and tried to think. The glare from the water was weak and ineffectual but reflected enough light to enable him to look up and search the ceiling for a way out. There wasn't. He wondered how long it would be before the water reached an overflow, if there was one. Meanwhile, the level was still rising. He tried to reach the pump again but it was still too far away. And even if he could bring it back up—what would he use for a collar? The original had fallen somewhere, and would be impossible to find in this situation. What the hell was Rogov doing?

He looked along the wall for other inspection panels and found one low enough so that when opened, it would act as an overflow. The immediate problem of flooding was over, and it would take twice as long for the water to reach his neck. That at least gave him time to think without hurrying.

He realised that with the lights, the airconditioning had also shut down, and that his air supply was limited. There was no point in trying to reckon out how many hours he had left—the true value could have probably been measured in minutes, anyway.

The water was by now edging towards his hips when it occurred to him that if he could find the sensor which operated the door lock he might be able to free it from the water and release the lock. But it could have been placed anywhere—and he didn't have that much time. He waded on to the end of the corridor and ripped the grille off the ventilators. They were too small for a man to go through. He waded back to the light source and tried to remember how high the water level had been when the sensor had shut everything down. About twenty centimetres, was his guess. And on the corridor walls—at that time the inside of the inspection panel space hadn't received any water flow.

He lowered himself to his knees, necessarily holding his breath and submerging his head below water, before looking for the sensor. In the weak light from the bulb he gave up and ran his fingers lightly over the walls. He managed to cover a metre before his lungs forced him back upright, gasping for air. This time he took several deep swallows, emptying his lungs completely before breathing in, and on the fourth dived back down. Another metre on and nothing. He felt cold and accidentally swallowed a little water. He had to press against the side of the walls to hold himself down and after just a few more centimetres forced himself upright, towards the water level. And stopped well under it. The water had gone well over his head.

In panic he scrambled about, till his hands found the inspection panel and he doubled up, thrust a foot into the hole, and pushed himself up, nearly knocking himself out when he finally reached the air pocket. Only a few inches deep, he gasped for air and fought the claustrophobia which arose around him like a ring of fire. Once he had calmed himself, he took several more deep breaths and dove again towards the floor.

This time he found it, fixed its position in his mind, and returned to the air pocket again. The available air was beginning to taste quite foul, and he had his deep breathing to blame for that. Besides which, a lot of air was dissolving in the water, bringing the level up—and not forgetting the oxygen he took from the air . . .

His next problem was to activate the sensor by reducing the pressure around it. He could do it by a frantic hand motion, but he doubted whether that would work. It was better than anything else he could think of, and besides, the air made him feel dizzy. He took a last deep breath and went down.

He took a few seconds out to find it again, then cupped his hands over it forming as perfect a seal as was possible, then suddenly brought the hands back.

For a second the lights flashed on, and he heard the groan of a motor start—and stop.

He lashed out in frustration at the door and found that there definitely was a current moving toward the seal. He blinked and saw that someone had forced a bar into the crack and as he watched the crack widened.

In a few seconds the water had reduced its level to well below his chest and he could breathe. A torch flashed into his eyes, and then over Leon's face.

"What the hell do we do now?" he asked.

Teld forced the door open wide enough to squeeze through and stood in the Computer Room. There were no systems operating and the water had risen to the level of his ankle. "I don't know," he replied, exhausted.

"We're locked in," Rogov reported. "All the controls are dead. We couldn't open the shelter entrance without them." He threw the torch on to the worktop and sat down. Teld picked up the torch and shone it on the computer room entrance. Well, at least the cubicles were on higher ground. He walked through and into the central hall. Someone grabbed him from the side and he started to struggle before a familiar voice said: "You're wet."

"You're right there," he agreed ruefully.

"What the hell happened?"

"I'm not saying anything here. Let's go into the office." Once there he hooked the torch on the wall and in the resulting half-light told her the story.

"Leaving us the problem of getting out," he finished. "I don't know how we'll do it but do it we must, and before the air goes stale. I didn't know the joints would be so delicate. That's what happened in the other shelter, except that being bigger, the inspection corridors would be partitioned off, creating effective bulkheads, which is why some places flooded, others didn't. Here, the system is all in one place. Besides, it's better the system's off. How would you like to be electrocuted? We're lucky it didn't happen when I opened the seal."

"Fourneir'll be over here as soon as he knows we're in trouble," she said. "We might not be able to do anything from this side but I'm damn sure he won't rest till everyone's out." There was a momentary silence while she thought. "I think he might ram the doors. They're made to withstand a fairly close shock-wave but not a direct hit."

"Or we might pump the water out of the Computer room," he said. "But the question would be finding the power source. Batteries—possibly, but they'd have to keep up a high output."

"Then you'd better get on with it," she said. "Or you'll have a riot on your hands out there."

"Correction—you'll have a riot on your hands. You were the one who was eager to assume complete command. Now you'll have to face up to the responsibilities."

"All right," she sighed.

* * *

Back in the computer room they lashed a pump together, but couldn't find an adequate power source.

"We could try osmosis," Teld suggested. "Perhaps the pressure differential would give us enough energy to drive it?"

"We couldn't rig a tank strong enough," said Rogov. "The pressures you could encounter are enormous."

"But we've got one," said Teld. "The main water tank."

"The lad's a genius . . . all right, what do you want me to do?"

"First off, gather all the sugar you can—"

"Not enough," Rogov replied. "You want a really concentrated solution—"

In the darkness, they both smiled.

* * *

The osmotic pump was an incredible success. The main water tank was empty. Once they reached it they were able to block the pipe with a collar and add a short hose over which was placed a semi-permeable membrane of treated latex. The pipe and hose were filled with water bailed from the surplus on the ground, in which the concentrate was dissolved—rapidly. After that, it was merely a wait of several hours while the water seeped through the membrane in a futile effort to dilute the concentrated solution in the tank. Futile because concentrate was added to the tank in a steady stream to maintain the normality. Rogov and Teld were justly proud of the development and as soon as the water level had fallen far enough they turned the power back on.

Except for a few systems which had fallen prey to the water flood and blew the second they were switched on, lighting, air and heat were back in operation—but most of all they could use the radio. They tried to raise Fourneir but the atmospheric interference was too great.

" Damned aurora must be right on top of us," Rogov decided. " Wish I could see it."

" I know how you feel," Teld replied wistfully. Most of the display screens had been damaged by the flood. Those still operating were just lines of interference.

Teld's finger hovered over the entrance release. What the hell, he thought, and brought the switch down. " Let's go and watch it," he suggested.

CHAPTER EIGHT

MOST OF the display screens in the Penthouse were still active and Teld rerouted satellite reception to them. They showed essentially the same as the shelter's screens, the central piece being the colourful Mercator projection with the deep red spots which denoted the blast area from nuclear bombs.

The wallscreen was still in operation but Teld didn't activate it. He was busy at the terminal when the other scientists walked in, and took their usual places round the table. When they were all settled, Fourneir stood up and rested his arms against the table. "It looks as though we've been very lucky indeed," he said. "I don't know about anyone else here but I for one didn't think that I would ever see this place again. However, we've been proved wrong. Today sees a new civilisation. One which has lived through the nuclear fires and must no longer be afraid of them. Whatever the figures of death and destruction in the history books, we must remember that however fierce the War had been, it at least left a few people round the world alive." He sat down and began to polish his glasses. " I think it would be a good idea if someone gave us an idea of just how badly the world is off. Michelson, what can you tell us?"

Michelson glanced at the notes he had brought with him. " It will go down as the shortest war on record," he began. " It lasted fifteen hours from the moment the first missile was launched to the second the last one fell. I've got a lot of statistical data I won't go into just yet but the main facts are these. The worst hit areas are undoubtedly the United States and Russia, which in a sense is but fair, since they started it. Of the two, the United States is the more severely crippled, having undergone a terrific bombardment before a third of its retaliatory missiles could leave their silos. That third, however, was still sufficient to bring down Russia to almost the same level of disablement. China also added her strike force to the destruction, with both hits in America and Russia while she suffered only minor relative damage."

" Do you think there'd be any organisation left in those countries?" Fourneir asked.

" On the military level, yes," Michelson replied. " One thinks, for instance, of the number of ships and submarines at sea which are untouched by the bombs but who won't open contact yet with the rest of the world because they fear their positions may be plotted and their vessels attacked with whatever hardware is left operable. I should imagine everything at sea will be returning to their bases to find out what is going on. Therefore it is reasonable to presume that the main responsibility of civil government will lie with the armed forces.

There's no reason to suppose that ambitious generals will take this opportunity to stage a coup or a number of them to gain possession of what is still the richest country in the world, although it must be admitted the possibility still exists. Very few cities were damaged, most of the targets were missile complexes and key military bases. The centres of government and administration look as though they've been severely blasted, but whether any of the Presidential staff is still alive I can't tell you. The President himself was in Florida."

"Russia, however, was hit quickly, efficiently, and if you can use the word here, cleanly. Prime targets have just been blasted with almost clinical precision. Only a few peripheral outlying villages were touched by the blasts, and of course, Moscow itself. Satellite pictures show that the Russians have expected this war for some time and they had been evacuating their troops from the larger military bases out on practice manoeuvres in the countryside. Not all of them escaped but there is still a sizeable armed force behind the Iron Curtain which I think we should beware of. Their own country lies in ruins, and they are bound to think that the nuclear war has left Europe similarly incapacitated. Whether they try any invasion tactics or not can only be answered with time. Of course, we ourselves should definitely advise Brussels that borders be patrolled."

"I'll see what the Ministry has to say about that later," Fourneir said.

"Thank you. And China. Well, here we have a most puzzling thing. From what we can tell, Peking has been hit with a moderately sized bomb. China dealt out quite a bit of punishment on her own behalf, both to the Russians and the Americans. What state they're in now you can bet that it was responsible to the Chinese. However, at that moment the tracking satellite was just going behind the horizon and I wouldn't trust any information from that point on. If a salvo had been launched from one of the Sino-Russian border bases it would look very much like on trace, and also the reverse. We'll just have to speculate on that point."

" This, of course, leaves them in a very good position, neither America nor Russia dominate the earth, though Russia's main forces are probably still strong enough to cause a considerable amount of trouble. This leaves the way open for Chairman Len Tsi to order expansion into Russian territory—and from where he's sitting he can't lose. The border troops will probably be recalled to make up for the losses the Russians suffered under the bombardment, leaving the borders virtually unpatrolled. Once the Russian force has consolidated itself they'll then move back out—probably meeting the Red Army in Siberia. But China still has her nuclear weapons. If she uses them to flatten Russia we might have to take a step towards retaliation ourselves."

" And are we in a position for such?" Fourneir asked.

" Pretty much the same as China. We've suffered less than minimal loss, with just a small part of Germany being hit—from a faulty bomb, I think, that somehow evaded our missile screen. Centres of government and military administration were unaffected."

"To sumnate then. Everyone who had anything hit America. Russia spun off with the next greatest damage, while China seems to have suffered as much damage as we ourselves. India is another matter. There are a lot of hostile countries either side of her borders, and a few have nuclear capability. In five or six years the radioactive areas should be safe enough to recolonise, no later than that."

The telephone rang and Fourneir picked it up, eventually signalling the others to relax and that the call would take a long time. Teld and Rogov left the table and looked out of the wallscreen. In the distance they could see one of the jets take off, curve away into the cloud and disappear.

"Do you think things are as simple as Michelson makes them out to be?" Rogov asked.

"I don't think so. You know how difficult it will be for other powers to resist thinking that this is their chance to expand a little sideways. It was only Russia and America who were keeping the world peace with their own separate blocs and of course the bomb. We haven't been on the scene long enough to consider ourselves a stabilising factor of any importance. In fact, we were part cause of the war. During the next ten years there'll be hundreds of small wars and I doubt whether you'd recognise a political map of the world this time next year."

"Seems as if the Van Allen belts are finally clear," Leighton said. "We're ready to take some prints." Rogov walked over to the terminal and began to punch out code-groups with sadistic force on the terminal. Teld continued to stare out of the window, thinking about the coming battles.

At first he didn't hear his name being called but eventually he turned round. Rogov held out some prints to him. "Will you look at these?" the Slav asked.

They looked like the normal colour prints one saw in the morning papers, showing the earth in its last quarter as a slice from a multi-coloured children's ball. The patterns were incomprehensible.

"I don't see what you want me to see," Teld replied.

"Look at North America," Rogov requested, outlining the east coast with his finger. Teld's eyes travelled along the print till they reached the fringes of what appeared to be a vast dustcloud. "Is this it?" he asked, indicating the cloud.

Rogov nodded. "I can't make head or tail of it," he said. "I've never seen anything like that before."

"What is it?"

"Some kind of thundercloud," Rogov said.

"Aren't they usual after a nuclear blast?"

"Yes, but not so bloody huge."

"That's a pretty unscientific description," Teld replied. "They could be dustclouds, in any case."

"Perhaps," Rogov replied, worriedly. "However, I'll get in touch with the weather stations, they're bound to know more about it."

He pre-empted the telestat and began work. Teld took the photos over to the workbench and looked at them under the laser stereo. The whole picture jumped at him into relief. For a moment, he was dizzied by the sense of altitude it gave him. After his eyes got used to the feeling, he began to examine more thoroughly the cloud. There were definitely concentration areas, he noticed towards the centre, just before the whole picture darkened before the earth's terminator. He moved his eyes back over the page to the coast, where a few shining concrete buildings could be just made out at highest magnification. That cloud could be significant—while on the other hand, it might disperse in a few hours. In either case, it was centred in America, three thousand miles or more distant.

"They haven't any weather ships that far out," said Rogov after he'd contacted the Weather Centre, clearing house for all meteorological information. "It looks as though I'll have to wait until the satellite comes over the terminator. Another three quarters of an hour. What do you think of it?"

Teld shrugged. "Whatever it is, it can't be much fun to encounter. Isn't there anything you could use in space?"

"The platform's not in the right place," Rogov pointed out. "And I don't know of anything else up there manned unless the Russians or Americans fired something before the war. In which case they won't contact us. But I could have the weather satellite's orbit changed." He snapped his fingers. "Why not? The observatory's not doing anything."

"The telescope's too big," Teld replied. "You could chance its position but the pix you'll get will be worse than useless. And the other equipment on board is too sensitive to use."

" Looks like the platform, then," Rogov said resignedly, turning back to the Stat. Fourneir, having completed his phone call, wandered over to see what was going on. Teld showed him the photographs and explained what he was trying to do.

" I doubt whether he'll do it," Fourneir said, shaking his head. " I know the man who runs the unit. A fanatical astronomer. He'd never consent to such a thing."

" We could always go through Brussels."

" True, but I don't like going over someone's head to our common masters, it always results in making more enemies whenever we play politics. Besides, this is so relatively unimportant, that I'd not take the risk anyway."

" Do you know what caused it?" Rogov asked from the telestat.

" No, but then, I'm no meteorologist," Fourneir replied. " And neither are you. It would be a far better idea to hand the problem over to someone who could solve it."

" I just have," Rogov said, " And they couldn't explain it away, either."

" If you think it's that important," Fourneir said. " But don't involve us in it."

" Don't worry," Rogov muttered. He walked over to the phone and dialled a number, overseas by the length, Teld judged. After a few seconds the amp clicked on. " Hello? Is that Dr. Guille?"

" Of course it is," he said. " What do you want, whoever you are?"

" Rogov," the Slav said. " I was wondering whether I could have the use of the orbiting telescope for a couple of hours—"

No, Teld thought to himself. Fourneir started to say something, but subsided. But his eyes shouted: I thought I told you to leave the old boy alone.

" Couple of hours?" Guille echoed. " What do you mean?"

" There would be a course correction involved—"

" That satellite is involved in important research work. Rhysler's Quark Theory must be substantiated with facts—"

" Dr. Guille, unless you've been hiding in a convent this past week—"

" Yes, yes, yes, I know all about the war," Guille replied testily. " But the research must go on. I'm sorry. I cannot authorise your use of the satellite."

" But the weather stations I am using are past the terminator now, and besides, they haven't the equipment I need to—"

" You want to use an observatory to take weather pictures? You must be out of your mind."

" If I show you what I've got on record would you think of changing your mind?" Rogov pleaded. He took a sheaf of photos and held them up in front of the screen, and as more of the photos were slapped face down on the desk after being shown Guille's face softened and finally developed an interested frown.

" I'll admit there is something unusual going on," said Guille. " But your own satellites will be over the area again soon." He made up his mind. "Call me again after you get some more photographs. If they prove to be interesting, then I'll consider your proposal." He cut the contact swiftly. Rogov leaned back in his chair and breathed out.

"I wish you'd be a little more tactful sometimes," Fourneir said uncomfortably. "Guille has a lot of pull in Brussels, and I don't want the reputation of the department suffering from the misdirected actions of just one member." But he smiled and added, "You've got him interested anyway."

The requested weather pix arrived promptly on time and Rogov spent a few minutes going over them by himself before letting anyone else take a look. "You can see that the cloud is much larger than we had imagined," he said. "And it's also travelled further out towards the east." It was true. The coast was almost completely covered. "The more I look at these the more worried I am."

Guille was telexed copies of the pix and together with Rogov they went over what the clouds could mean. "I know that we don't have much to do with meteorology," Guille pointed out, "but the Weather Bureau is always available for consultation and hasn't anything like the observatory in orbit."

"Then you'll do it?" Rogov asked.

"Yes," the Frenchman said. "I had the course corrections computed a few moments ago." He grinned. "I didn't want you to think you were getting it all your own way. However, there are ways and means of dealing with this. We could always arrange to have a plane run over the storm—"

"You forget the sensitive political situation," Rogov pointed out. "It would be shot down in seconds."

Guille nodded. "In that case . . . well, we have several astronomers here who work on their own independent projects. One of them is an expert on Jovian matters. If it is a storm it is a storm of incredible size and certainly worth his while to study. Perhaps he might be able to tell us something."

While Guille was gone in pursuit of the astronomer Rogov turned to Teld. "You can go, if you like." Almost everyone else had left the Penthouse, except for Fourneir, and he was packing his briefcase.

"I'm staying where I am," said Teld doggedly. "Even if only to make sure you don't start World War Four."

Guille appeared on the screen. "My assistant is waiting to patch into the satellite. Would you like an open data feed between our computers?"

"I don't know," Rogov said. "Ours uses a special programming technique." He cut the sound. "Teld, would you like to stay and translate between the two systems? I know it's going to be a heavy job, and it's getting quite late, but this looks important—"

"Don't bother," said Teld fatalistically. "I'll do it."

"Thank, thanks very much. Hello, Guille? Good. Well, I've arranged everything this end. When could you start sending data through?"

Teld found a pen and paper, and sat down behind

the terminal. Fourneir gave them both an incredulous look, shook his head and left.

* * *

The wallscreen had darkened and seen the moon rise and set while the stars passed in lordly majesty over the Complex and the heads of the two scientists still working in the Penthouse. Teld didn't feel at all tired—he was more shocked by the size of the pile of papers lying half in and out of the waste bin than by the time when he finally gave himself a few moments to clear his eyes and stretch his writing hand, the wrist of which was aching. I use a typewriter too much, he told himself and looked over to where Rogov was stifling a tired yawn and trying to input the programmes lying by the side of the terminal. Prints taken by the observatory were lying scattered over the conference table. Teld stood up, stretched and sat on the edge of the tabletop, looking at the different stages the thunderstorm had gone through.

Or thunderstorms. The cloud, which covered twenty states and was by now well out into the Atlantic Ocean was not just a formation of rubble and dust formed by the nuclear blasts, but a tremendously powerful storm with what looked like dark spiral galaxies at the centre but which were, or so Teld had been informed, tornadoes. In front and to the rear of the central group of perhaps a dozen were smaller groups of spirals, which had been observed to break up and then reform. These were made under infra red radiation, but the tornadoes were shown with better clarity in the lidar—a laser ' radar '—pix.

Here, the cloud was a thin, filmy haze over the tornadoes themselves. The concentrations were shown to be spread over a ' corridor ' through which they moved thirty miles wide in places. The other photographs showed the electrical density of the cloud, magnetrospheric, and lidar. " There's a hell of a lot of radio noise coming from it," Rogov told him. " The thunderbolts must be of the multimegavolt order at least. But it's not the thundercell I'm worried about, at least, not primarily. It's the tornadoes that bother me."

Guille came back on to the line. " We should have speed vectors and detailed analyses ready within the hour," he said. " I've one of the Bureau's weatherships, called the *Ilumvalle*, I think. Other ships in the Atlantic have been ordered out of the immediate area. It's a pity we haven't any submarines attached on to the department. However, we'll just have to do the best with the little we have." He sighed. " It will be interesting to watch the evolution of the storm. A pity we can't gather information more directly."

" Couldn't you drop a probe through ?" Teld asked.

Guille blinked. " We could. If they can survive the turbulent Venusian atmosphere they can certainly make it through ours. But we only have two on the platform. Are you suggesting we drop nearly half a billion dollars worth of equipment down ?"

" No need, one will do the trick," Rogov said.

" I will get in touch with Brussels," said Guille. " They will do this thing for me, I think."

" You could strip away most of the shielding," Rogov added, " leaving just the ablatives, which could be junked after re-entry. That would give it more time on the way down."

" We could do even better with drogues fitted," Guille said.

Teld shook his head. " I doubt whether you'd have the time to install them. Besides, they'd bounce around like table tennis balls, from one level to another. All you really need is a cross section on film. Something that size won't last long. I'll give it another day and it'll have died out."

" Very well. I'll have them launched as soon as possible. You know, it's just occurred to me that we could reduce the weight still further if we took some of the radio gear. The *Ilumvalle* could act as a booster relay station as well."

" Good idea," said Rogov. " If that's that, then you can call us when the sensors can be dropped." He rested and switched off the screen. " You know, I think it's high time we had some sleep."

Teld shrugged. " I'm not particularly tired."

" I know," he nodded. " It gets you that way sometimes. I doubt whether I'd sleep anyway with that thing on my mind. To be honest, it should have dispersed hours ago—Guille's assistant couldn't believe that it lasted so long. But they know more about that than I do. I can't puzzle out what caused it, though."

" The bombing surely," Teld said.

" Yes, that must be right, but how?" He pulled on a

newly lit cigarette and watched the star patterns in the wallscreen.

A few seconds later the stat began to print more pictures from the satellite.

CHAPTER NINE

CAPTAIN VAN SEERD was not too pleased when he received Guille's orders to turn his ship around and sail as far to the south-east as he could without, in his estimation, endangering the lives of his crew or the ship. A few moments later he was given details of the storm and what he was expected to do within those limitations.

After reading the orders brought to his cabin by the steward he hit back angrily at the thick-headedness of land-based admirals. "You'd better ask the radioman for confirmation of this," he ordered. "What they think this ship is called? NS *Pingpong*?"

The steward did his best to conceal his smile and hurried back to the radio room along the bright corridors of the ship. As soon as the steward had closed the door van Seerd stood thinking, then came to an abrupt decision and shrugged on his jacket and cap, but not bothering to shave the three-day long stubble on his cheeks and chin. Van Seerd was not a strict disciplinarian, and he knew better than to waste time which could be valuable on cosmctic surgery except when the opposite sex were concerned—and trapped out here in the Atlantic, a thousand miles from the nearest shore, he was in no danger of running into eligible spinsters. And besides, however he felt about the chair-warmers in Brussels, they were his bosses, and if they thought he should turn the ship and risk his friends and himself—but more important, the ship—then he was duty bound to sail into the very jaws of Cerberus, if need be and they presented themselves. Besides, he would take no risks in any case. Not on *his* salary—

When he reached the bridge, the helmsman reported the ship's position and went back to his navigational duties. On the latest up-to-date vessels, of which the Nuclear Ship *Ilumvalle* was one, very little crew were needed. Just the captain, his valet who doubled as cook, the chief engineer, and the navigator. Nothing else. Computer pilots and advanced visual aids while servomechanisms did the menial jobs of keeping the ship clean were responsible for the actual command of the ship. The humans were simply there to tell the machines what to do, and when necessary, repair them.

Van Seerd was contemporary enough to realise the desirability and efficiency of such techniques and systems, and worked with the machines without any feeling of abnormality at all. Not like many old salts who regarded the computer and the men who ran it as effeminated dehumanised freaks in their traditionally chauvinistic attitude. If their view of the computer plumbed the depths of their extensive profanity, then the advent of small nuclear drives for even the lowliest vessel must leave them speechless. As far as van Seerd was concerned, steam driven ships went out with the coracle, and the few being used nowadays for ocean travel were nothing more than antiquities not worth the price of the expensive ticket for a journey which in a nuclear liner would not take a third the time. There was also the solidarity which oceanauts and astronauts shared. Both their ' ships ' were driven by nuclear piles and spent long months in the space between ports. And steamships were dirty, smelly, and far too dangerous to operate. Suppose a boiler blew? He shuddered at the thought. Or of having to cope with funnel drag? With the advent of classes such as the *Ilumvalle,* sailing became a science, not a chore. Of course, the important skills of navigating, oceanography, and the essential understanding of psychology which made a sailor a captain were still needed, but the pressures of steam-life were no longer around.

In addition to the normal crew of four, there were seven scientists who manned the equipment which had been built into the midship. They were all meteorologists, and the *Ilumvalle* had been commissioned especially to be fitted with this ' new ' equipment. During the war the scientists made veiled—and not so veiled—hints that once the conflict ended they should immediately go to the nearest Continental port, which van Seerd had ignored. In fact, during the war they had seen several ICBMs sail overhead, leaving their rocket's ice-trails far behind them but otherwise invisible. And once, far away, an American nuclear submarine had surfaced, looked them over, and decided to submerge itself again without making any contact at all. That had been a very tense moment, when they first noticed the bows breaking the surface, then the conning tower, and finally the hull came into view, and there the submarine was, riding the waves, a huge black mythical sea monster with their lives or death in its torpedo tubes. Through the binoculars it could be seen that the missile silo covers were stained brown by the heat of lift-off. After a while, its curiosity sated, it slid back under the waves as silently as it had surfaced.

At the bridge he called Dr. Sallenburg, the expedition leader—in as much as they seemed to have one—to tell him the glad news.

" What is it, Captain ?" Sallenburg asked.

" Looks like you've got your wish," van Seerd replied. " We're going back towards that storm of yours."

There was a moment's silence as Sallenburg digested the news. " Who ordered this ?" was his question.

" Brussels. I don't intend to stay there any longer than necessary so I thought I'd phone now to let you get your equipment ready. The plan is to drop some sort of probe through the storm level, which will transmit messages to us. We will transmit the messages to the W.B. in Europe."

There had been a certain amount of rivalry and distance between the scientists and crew when they first stepped on board but three months at sea together had cooled this to friendship. Once it had been understood that their functions were so different as to preclude any rivalry and that whatever Sallenburg might have to say, van Seerd was the only Captain, they mixed and talked freely. In fact, they learnt a lot from each other, both about their work and themselves.

The navigator gave him a course which would take them within observation distance of the storm without leaving them in danger of being overtaken. Van Seerd checked the course himself and while he had a great deal of faith in the *Ilumvalle* he didn't believe for a moment that it was unsinkable, as the builders claimed. They would be heading towards conditions which far exceeded the parameters laid down that marked the ship's durability. He didn't want to go closer than twenty miles from the outer edge of the storm. While the navigator was feeding the course into the computer pilot Sallenburg walked on to the bridge. Outside the weather was typical storm—dark clouds and heavy rain. Luckily no part of the ship couldn't be reached through direct access corridors. He examined the course proposed and nodded. " I agree with you," he said. " But your limit might well be within the edge of the storm itself."

" If it is we can always cancel it," van Seerd replied. " I don't intend to risk the ship."

Sallenburg scratched at his unruly hair. " Well, they are probably depending on direct observation in any case," he decided. " Otherwise they'd just want us to boost the probe's signals. I'd better roll out the cine-cameras and find a few telescopes. In fact, we might find that we could possibly go a little closer in and not suffer much more than getting our faces wet . . ."

" Doctor," van Seerd replied flatly, " I was told to proceed to the point where in my estimation, Doctor, not yours or anyone else's, the danger factor was negligible. You can prattle on about how men of science must not let personal fear interrupt their ceaseless search for knowledge but as you know, I'm captain and not a man of science. Any more talk about changing course and I'll make you walk the plank."

Sallenburg smiled. "Don't you mean you'll make me walk a metal plate at the point of a rivet gun?"

* * *

Liefmann, Sallenburg's assistant, slapped the side of the terminal before him disgustedly. "An opportunity like this comes up once every lifetime," he said. "And what happens—we have to be right in the middle of the action with out of date equipment and a leaking tub."

Sallenburg rubbed the bridge of his nose. "I know what you mean, Carl, but you can hardly call the lidar and computers out of date. All right, they're a few months old and a new generation may well have been developed since then but they're still adequate for our purposes. And the *Ilumvalle* is decidedly not leaking. We'll be returning to base for a refit in another couple of weeks in any case."

Sallenburg doubted whether they would be refitted when they finally berthed. The war would have removed much of the priority from the weatherships to the military services and when they reached dry land it could be for the rest of their lives.

The sea was decidedly getting rougher as they sailed

to meet the storm, and after three months Sallenburg was sufficiently able to feel the minute disturbance that not even the gyroscopes could mask. The probe would be dropped at eleven thirty to meet the storm at approximately twelve hundred hours. It would spend just over ninety seconds falling through the storm, gathering and broadcasting information before it hit the sea and sank down to whatever fate was awaiting it in the depths.

"We've entered the disturbance area, in another hour or so we should be emplaced," Sallenburg said. It was only nine hundred hours now. They had a clear two hours to make the journey. "What have you got on the storm so far?"

"Well, it seems to be the biggest storm on record. I couldn't believe the report till I checked the figures myself. You can see the lidar chart for yourself. As a matter of fact, I was able to go over some of the old records we have, just prior, during, and immediately after the bombing of North America and the storm itself started in the Midwest—which received the heaviest bombardment—and reached the east coast in under fourteen hours, which indicates a forward speed of one hundred and thirty miles an hour."

Sallenburg whistled. "That's about twice as fast as normal," he said.

Leifmann nodded. "With the size and the number of central tornadoes it must be incredibly destructive. Crossing America it must have wreaked more havoc than the bombing. Certainly absolutely nothing could have been left standing in its path."

" Another thing I noticed was that after the radio noise from the ionosphere had died down there was still a great deal of disturbance which played around with our instruments. I've tracked this to the storm itself. That thundercell must have a tremendous charge. Of course, interference isn't unknown with most normal storms, but this is completely off the scale compared with anything we've had before."

" Strong enough to drown out the probe signals?" Sallenburg asked.

Leifmann spread his hands helplessly. " No way of telling till it starts transmitting," he said.

Sallenburg considered the situation. " I wonder if, in fact, van Seerd realises the seriousness of the storm?"

" The seas must be telling him," Leifmann replied.

* * *

Van Seerd looked out over the ship's bows and sensed the fury of the storm. He could see the thunderclouds ahead, stretching right over the horizon and to either side as far as he could see. With binoculars there was still no end to the black smudge. Over the ship, the sky was grey, but had stopped raining a little while ago. Occasionally lightning would flash down from the tormented skies and pick out the sea in its ghostly blue-white light. Once he had doubted the reports he had received from the station in Brussels. Now he was not so sure. It was difficult to deny the picture the lidar painted. But there was still the nagging voice in his mind telling him that the storm belonged to some seventeenth- or eighteenth-century novel about the sea containing grisly paragraphs describing sea-snakes and exotic, man-eating plants. Confronting the reality was like coming face-to-face with Moby Dick. But he certainly did not intend to do battle with this.

The trouble, he knew, lay in the fact that the probe was vital and its radio range was limited. A last minute change of plan in Brussels and it was decided that the probe would transmit its information in 'squirt' maser transmission. In this case, the data would be condensed into a single, short, but powerful broadcast aimed directly at the ship in the form of a cone, with the vertex originating at the probe and the controlled incoherency of the beam enveloping the ship with the transmitted signal. They had to be at the right place at the right time, or the probe would have been wasted, and they only had two. The exercise was proving to be tremendously expensive for someone.

What was worse, the storm was acting on his radio so that the closer he came to the storm epicentre, the less perfect his contact with the weather station. The lidar was unaffected—the pulses being too strong to be drowned out by the lightning. Well before they reached the twenty mile radio limit radio contact was lost. "How do you intend to relay the information signal from the probe?" he asked Sallenburg.

"The same way as we receive it," the scientist replied. "By maser signal. It'll take a few minutes to set up the equipment but we should be finished long before the probe reaches her target."

"How long before we're in place?" van Seerd asked the navigator.

"Another eight minutes," the dour Nederlander replied. "In fifty-one minutes the probes will be launched, and should start transmitting the first maser squirts at three second intervals after that immediately. But we can ignore the signals received while she's in the upper atmosphere."

Van Seerd nodded and stood brooding over the black thunderclouds ahead, yearning to know how it had been created, and what was needed to destroy it. Through his field glasses he could see that the sea ahead of the ship was extremely turbulent and dark. What would it be like at the centre of the vortex? he asked himself. They were heading towards the storm at an acute angle, so that if it suddenly changed direction, they would not be faced with having to suddenly reverse and waste time losing their forward momentum. And the only danger this far out would not be the hundred and thirty mile an hour winds but the seas themselves, overcoming the stabilisers and tipping the ship.

He was still in the same position, with the same look in his eyes, when the navigator looked up from the chart table and said: "Captain, the probe has been launched." The voice broke him from his trance, and he nodded absently to acknowledge the news.

By the time the probe began transmission, they were centred in the broadcast cone and were receiving beautifully clear signals as the machine arrowed down through the atmosphere towards the dark mass. There was a certain attractiveness about it, van Seerd thought, a destructive power he couldn't comprehend but only admire, an exhibition of nature's horrific might. He felt compulsed to go nearer to the storm, to pilot his ship through the secondary whirlwinds towards the awesome tornadoes, to reach out and touch them, almost. Wondering how far he could go, whether he could just touch the point at which the storm would catch and smash his ship without pausing. It was the most seductive thing he had ever experienced. Coming out from the fascination and back to his normal state of mind came as something of a shock, but some small part of him still wanted to order the ship to close in. But he daren't bargain with his ship and crew for a ringside seat.

* * *

The probe entered the earth's atmosphere in an almost leisurely fashion. It had been sighted and launched on a curving elliptic arc which would bring it through the epicentre of the storm and in particular one of the dozen or or so central tornadoes designated CTF-8, by far the largest and most interesting.

As the density began to thicken around the probe the heatshield began to heat up, till it was a dull, angry red and then a fierce actinic white. At the same time the retrorockets fired and the two glows, one of incandescent gas, the other of metal, were indistinguishable. And then slowly the heatshield began to darken as the probe was decelerated, till its speed was too low for friction to melt the delicate parts hidden by the ablative screen, which was jettisoned as the probe arced over America towards the tornado. The two halves of the shield spiralled downwards towards the ground.

Unencumbered, the sensors on the probe could now start assembling information and coding it for maser transmission. The tiny computer on board adjusted the maser beam and then activated the transmitter. Three seconds later, another signal was sent, and again, three seconds after that.

On board the *Ilumvalle* the signals were recorded and then retransmitted across the sea to the weather station. Sallenburg looked at the tapedecks and wondered what he would find when he untangled the messages in them. The captain appeared to be inordinately interested in the tornadoes, something Sallenburg would never have thought could happen. The scientist could understand his own interest as scientific curiosity, but he didn't share the same viewpoint as van Seerd. Here was nature at her fearsome best, and all the scientists could do was sit around, measuring, analysing and otherwise ignoring the incredible beauty of nature run wild.

Sallenburg was more concerned about the captain's ability to keep the ship on an even keel without losing any part of the transmission from the probe. The ship was definitely pitching quite violently now to his sharpened senses. Even Leifmann, a confirmed landlubber who was more concerned by the lack of women than the joys of sailing, could feel the momentary shift and correction under his feet.

The probe reached her terminal velocity just before entering the upper regions of the thundercloud. Through maelstrom it fell, moving so fast that not even the winds had a chance to divert its path. It sliced through several more cloud layers before the vernier rockets, silent till this moment, flared briefly, aligning the probe with the centre of the tornado.

For a few moments, it cleared the lower cloud base and was in a region of almost neutral air-movement, the legendary eye of the tornado. Around it, the walls of the tuba shifted and in them tons of rubble still left over from the journey across the land whirled round before inevitably being thrown clear and into the sea. Then the moment was over as the probe passed into the funnel wall and out the other side, miraculously avoiding being hit by debris before the delicate instruments hit the sea and the water closed over the machine, rendering its short but active life irrevocably over.

Back on the *Ilumvalle* the destruction of the probe was noted when the signals ceased coming in. Sallenburg left the tapedecks running but they had all they would ever receive from the probe.

" You'd better tell the captain it's over," he said. " Then we'll start decoding the signals."

The Captain accepted the demise of the probe without comment. To him the tornado was still the same inexplicable phenomenon it had been ten minutes previously, and he knew that he would follow the report Sallenburg promised to send him after they had finished with the signals only with difficulty. Still, what did he care? He looked at the fury still raging twenty miles distant. It had showed no sign of breaking up, and would be there this time tomorrow, the next day, and the day after that. Whatever it was, it wasn't an ordinary storm. He ordered the navigator to bring them away from the disturbance and into clear seas.

For a moment it crossed his mind that the tornado might well live till it reached Europe. The thought was new to him, and terrifying in its implications. There had not been a tornado in the Continent for a great many years, and although they were by no means strangers in the land, none of the cities or towns had ever had to cope with such storms. He could imagine the devastation it would cause and felt the pang of fear. Would he return to his homeland and such destruction? He prayed not. He wondered what he would find when he returned to the Continent, but then, that would only be a few days in the future. They would not wait for the recall signal but follow the tornado to the friendly shores.

CHAPTER TEN

"THIS," SAID Fourneir, "is happening far too often for my liking." He looked round the Penthouse, at the disordered table tops and scattered papers. "When the hell are you going to leave this place in an organised state?"

"I assure you," Rogov replied with all his usual lack of respect, "I wouldn't have phoned you unless things were pretty desperate."

"So it's over the sea," Fourneir grunted. "What do you want me to do about it?"

"You don't understand the significance of the photographs we have?" Rogov asked. He held out a handful to the scientist, who took them and leafed through, holding out a couple for closer inspection.

It was true, he noticed gloomily. The tornado formation had moved over the sea and was heading east at the speed of two miles a minute. Of course, it still had two and a half thousand miles to cross, any time during which it might blow itself out, but that still made cause for concern. "What have you done about it?" he asked.

"Doctor Guille has authorised the use of a probe for

our experiment. We intend to drop the probe through the thundercloud and into one of the tornadoes itself, this one we've called CTF-8. If all goes well it should be ready for launch in two hours."

" Why so long ?" Fourneir demanded.

" The usual radio gear has been found unsuitable for purposes. The radio activity of the thunderstorm is so powerful it'll blanket any transmissions from the probe after entering the cloud. So we've decided to install a maser which'll give us a pulsed signal every three seconds, powerful enough to punch through the interference to a relay ship which should send us the signals direct. From there we can decode the signals and present a running commentary of the storm a few seconds after the probe experiences it."

" I hope you haven't panicked Brussels over this," Fourneir said.

" You're the only person outside of us three who knows in Europe, sir," Rogov said.

" Good. Well, it looks like we're back on the merry-go-round. I suppose you'll want to stay and see what happens. I thought as much. The both of you look like ' After the nervous breakdown '. Someone go and make me a cup of coffee." He settled down and began to search through the charts, photographs and scribble-pads on the table.

Despite the weather conditions, the relay from the weathership was clear and precise, and from a few seconds after the probe began transmitting, they had a clear view from the probe's cameras as it hurtled through the atmosphere till the ablative screen covered the camera lens. Not long afterwards the burst of light signalled that the heatshield had been discarded and they had a clear view of the earth from twenty miles up; in the distance the horizon curved sharply to either side and the blue haziness of the sky was streaked with white clouds. Almost second by second the unsteady image came closer and details of the land beneath could be made out—and then gone as the probe flew over the sea and towards the black mass of the thunderstorm directly ahead.

The probe's speed was by now five miles a second, and to slow the intricate machine down the retrorockets were fired once more. The image jarred, and then steadied as the rockets cut off and the probe took up its downward plunge. By the time it reached the cloud it was nearing its terminal velocity.

This was what it must have been like when the previous machines entered the Venusian atmosphere, Teld thought. The silver-grey clouds seemed to boil as they approached, sending wisps of vapour out into the sky. And then, suddenly, the probe was in the cloud and the mists closed around the cameras. Nothing could be seen except a vague luminescence occasionally relieved by the odd flash of lightning. The silver-grey colour gradually darkened to indigo before the probe broke through the base of the cloud and into the vortex.

They could see the funnel walls spiralling upwards towards the base of the thundercloud, the smokey-grey whirlpool of rubble and vapour, gradually lightening as the tornado cleared itself of the impurities it had picked up overland. The picture darkened again as the probe hit the funnel walls and Teld stared down into the section of dust and air till the probe burst once again to open air and enjoyed an instant of life till the water level rose to meet and smash the craft.

The Penthouse was silent except for the hum of the tapedecks and he stood up, moving away from the terminal to glare moodily through the wallscreen at the people moving below. Without saying anything to Fourneir he left the Penthouse.

Mel, surprisingly enough, was still in the flat, and looked him over critically when he sat down. "You look as though you could have done with the bath I just had," she said.

"You don't need a bath," he replied gallantly, falling into a loose sprawl.

"On the contrary," she denied. "I smelt terrible."

"I didn't notice anything," he added.

"You lie in your dentures," she said. "Between you and the shelter I didn't have time to brush my teeth, let alone powder my axillus. No woman could smell good after this last week."

"Then I'm lucky you haven't got bad breath. I'm tired and I want to know where you've hidden the sedatives."

"I have a feeling this is going to be one of those lifetimes—they're still in the overnight bag. Which is still in the shelter. But I've got a much better tranquilliser—you're having too many late nights, do you know that? From now on I'm making up your mind for you . . ." Her voice tailed off. She was preaching to one asleep. " See you later," she murmured resignedly and left him to his dreams, or nightmares.

* * *

They let him sleep through till late that afternoon, and then mercilessly awoke him from the land of slumber and returned him to the world of the horribly real. Fourneir promised him information on the one hand and threatened with the other. Teld stood dizzily on his feet and tried to wash the tiredness out with a shower before shrugging on his clothes and telling Fourneir he was on his way.

" Don't take too long," Fourneir said.

" I'll take as long as I bloody like," Teld replied, and cut the link. The satisfaction this produced was minimal, so he walked out of the flat still with a temper.

Rogov arrived back at much the same time. " He won't leave us alone, will he?" Rogov snapped under his breath in the lift. " Christ, I've hardly had any sleep."

" It was our own fault," Teld said. " There was a cot in the Penthouse. Either one of us could have used it—"

" Oh, stop defending him," Rogov replied wearily. " I've just about had my fill of this place. The sooner the storm arrives, the better. It should have been knocked down years ago."

During the next hour, he yawned prodigiously, not bothering to cover his mouth, much to the annoyance of

Michelson, and the amusement of the others. Teld glanced at the output from the computer, then focused his eyes and began again. This time round the figures, no longer blurred, made sense. Someone handed him hangover pills—they would at least clear his head, though at the expense of his stomach, which almost cheerfully tied itself in excruciating knots of agony as his body reacted to the pills.

Fourneir cleared his throat and adopted his lecture-platform manner. "Now, first to the physical details of the storm," he said, looking at the four scattered round the table. "The thundercloud can be regarded as one large thundercell, with a diameter of sixy miles, under which the tornadoes, or as I've named these particular models, tornids—you'll see why in a moment. On with the thundercell, though. The turbulence created by the tornids though, through cross winds acting with each other, have created secondary thundercells some distance from the primary cell, giving the whole storm an effective radius of one fifty miles, and an area of ninety thousand miles. Yes, gentlemen—it's that big.

"Now to the tornids. I doubt whether you're familiar with the theory behind their formation so here goes. An ordinary tornado is formed when the base of the thundercloud it belongs to revolves fast enough to create a like-moving current in the air below it, which then extends down to the ground and picks up dust and other debris which gives it its characteristic colour. These tornadoes move across land or sea in a general eastern direction before blowing themselves out and having left a path of destruction behind. Often they last for several days but the life varies. Some just come and go within a short period of time. Not a lot about them is known even now, despite heroic efforts on the behalf of American Universities to find a solution to this problem which mostly affects the Americans. Now, however, it affects us. The pattern of creation is the only common point the tornids and conventional tornadoes share. The latter have a forward speed of anything up to seventy miles an hour while the rotational speed value is usually a maximum of five hundred. Our tornids move at one thirty miles an hour and their rotational velocity is in excess of twelve hundred. They are half a mile wide and there are an estimated thirteen under the primary cell, where the charge is concentrated. Their effect is so violent they have created whirlwinds of tornado dimensions both in front and to the rear of the primary cell. These are short-lived but every bit as violent due to their cluster-shapes of five to seven tornadoes each.

"The thirteen tornids form the group we've called Central Tuba Formation, down through the most violent member a small interplanetary probe was dropped which gave us this information. Now, the question we must ask ourselves is whether this storm will eventually blow itself out and leave us in peace, or reach the other side of the Atlantic—our side—and continue on its way east over our continent?"

"Did you say hit Europe?" Rogov asked, suddenly awake and alert.

Fourneir nodded. "Yes. I'm afraid that's right. So

far, since we've been monitoring it, there hasn't been the slightest indication that the force of the storm has in any way diminished during its trip across the ocean. Rather, in fact—" he paused, as if taking a deep breath to get through the next quickly and without incident "—there is a basis for suggesting that the CTF has grown somewhat."

"That's a little hard to believe," said Leighton, slowly.

Fourneir held up a hand. "Please. I'm going to go on to that topic in a moment. Much more important now is the projected path of the storm. As I've said, it is continuing east and will eventually cross Northern Britain, over the North Sea—and through Southern Scandinavia."

"Ah," said Leighton.

"Naturally, Brussels have been informed and are taking steps to evacuate the Complex before the storm arrives. We've had a general warning out to cities and towns in the storm's path but as you can appreciate, either the warnings'll be ignored, or else acted on with hysteria. Whether the Authorities will do anything to help evacuation I can't tell you, but the geodesic domes are being brought down and removed as quickly as possible. The storm's ETA is just under twelve hours from now."

There was a very uncomfortable silence after the speech. Nobody wanted to add anything to what Fourneir had said, and were reluctant to ask for further information. What they had just heard was bad enough. Fourneir finally broke the silence by retaking the floor. "Ah, I believe Mitch has a few words to explain the formation and state of the tornadoes, don't you?"

Mitch nodded and rose to his feet. " What I'm about to tell you is pure speculation, of course, but under the circumstances it's the only theory forthcoming and seems to hold water pretty well. We take as our starting point the nuclear bombardment of North America. It was hit pretty thoroughly, and the bombs were detonated almost simultaneously as far as we're concerned.

" As you're aware, thunderclouds are pretty familiar features of nuclear tests, but they don't normally amount to much and die out after unloading the static charge of the thundercell. But think of how that thundercell is formed. When the bomb is detonated, several million cubic metres of air is suddenly flashheated and pushed right through the atmosphere, and with dust forms the famous mushroom cloud. However, the heat also brings warm dry air up to meet cold wet air, forming the thundercell, around the base of the mushroom cloud. The classic formation of the thundercell. But here the bombs were well in the fifty megaton range and there were many of them. Naturally, under such ferocious conditions, the tornadoes formed, the air currents excited by the fast rotation of the thundercloud bases. But these particular tornadoes were fundamentally different in that their size and power was big enough to create new thundercells, or recharge the old one, as it moved. Air is sucked into the funnel, or ' tuba ' as the meteorologists so aptly name them, dried and warmed by its passage up towards the base of the thundercloud. Once again, the classic conditions for the formation of thundercells. Of course, all this time the thundercell is discharging itself and the heat loss through every level of the cycle is tremendous—I doubt whether under normal conditions the system would be five per cent efficient—but in this case, with the cell being recharged continuously, and of course, with so many tornadoes feeding dry air up to the condensation level, it would appear that the thundercell is charging itself faster than the forked lightning we see in these photographs discharges it.

"The system would appear to be self-supporting, growing every minute in its size and destructive capability. It is not too difficult to envisage a time in the near future when the storm, having travelled round the world once already, starts its journey again but this time extending itself as far south as the equator. Naturally, the more it passes over humid seas the faster it will grow, and as you all know, the seas cover two thirds of the earth's surface. In time earth will resemble the planet Venus from space with a thick envelope of turbulent vortices raging round the globe, covering every detail of the land from then until the sun grows cold."

"But surely," said Teld, "once the thundercloud reaches a mountain range, won't the tubas be forced to climb the sides of the mountain till they reach the cloud-base itself?"

"Perhaps the tornadoes, but not the cloud. You see, the thundercell will ride the cold air currents up and over the summit and start anew over the other side. Besides, the cloud will cover the area over the mountains and beyond. If it does have any effect on the overall structure of the cloud it will be purely local and short-lived." He paused. "This is certainly a worthy and respectable daughter of the temperate zone storms which occur on the planet Jupiter, which had been the first destination of the probe successfully launched from the platform."

"So wherever we go, it'll get us," Rogov sumnated.

"That is my considered opinion," Michelson said. "There is no way to disperse the cloud with chemicals sprayed from above by planes. You can check the figures for yourselves. However, there is one slight chance."

Everyone leaned closer. "What's that, Michelson?" Fourneir demanded.

"The fact of the matter is that several years ago a chemical was developed which promised to help dampen the force of hurricanes and tornadoes. This organic substance was sprayed on to the seas where it formed a thin layer one molecule thick. The idea was to suppress wave motion and prevent evaporation through which a tornado such as ours receives energy through latent heat when the vapour condenses into rain. Tests showed that despite the fact it slightly increased the windspeed by calming the surface motion of the sea, the chemical was a tremendous success. Now if our resources could be directed towards producing enough of the chemical to cover the wave action of the seas, it would eventually slow the hurricane down. But we must remember that here we face the choice between two evils. We could never possibly destroy all the slick after it has succeeded—if it succeeds at all—in destroying the tornadoes. And they could never hope to do this for many years."

" It looks as though we're faced with destroying by our own hands everything we've built up in this continent by careful planning through gearing everything towards the destruction of the tornado, while if we delay we'll see it smashed regardless." Fourneir fiddled with his pen. " I'd better call Brussels over this."

" You know what they'll say in advance," Michelson pointed out. " They'd never authorise such a thing. They would rather wait it out."

" Perhaps," Fourneir agreed unhappily. " But on the other hand they must be made aware of the choice."

He was only a few minutes in conversation. When he had finished he placed the receiver down carefully and turned to face the others. " You were right about the chemical experiments, Mitch," he said. " But the experts in Brussels say that they found evaporation was increased by the suppression of surface evaporation. They agree that it could work under special conditions. But before they commit themselves to working on the problem they want to know more about the CTF."

" How will they do that?" Rogov asked.

" Quite simply, by leaving the problem to us. Someone is going to have to stay behind and see the tornado through in the shelter."

There was a long silence. " Do you think it'll work?" Leighton asked.

" It might. In any case, we don't seem to have much choice. They don't want to risk any of their experts by flying him up here. Most of the work'll have to be done by one of us with nothing but the computer."

Rogov gestured upward with his thumb. "This building won't last long in that storm."

"No, but the computer is down there," Fourneir replied, indicating the floor. "And there is in my mind a good chance that both the shelter and the machine will come through without too much damage."

"The only question now, is, of course, who stays."

"It's going to be very tricky solving that one," Michelson said. "How do you intend to do it?"

"I don't. I'm going to ask for volunteers."

"You think anyone'll volunteer to do that?" Rogov exploded. "You must all be mad." He stood looking at their startled faces, then shook his head and left.

"Well, that seems to leave him out of the final picking," said Fourneir. "Now, before we wind up, is there anyone else who would like to storm out abruptly?"

* * *

"You're crazy!" Mel shouted. "What the hell persuaded you to do a thing like that? You're not in your right mind."

"Somebody has to do it," he reminded her.

"Then let somebody else do it," she replied. "Christ—why do I put up with you?" She sat down on the end of the bed and lit a cigarette. Her luggage bags were lying stacked against the wardrobe and in the distance, they could hear the drone of transports arriving for the evacuation.

"Look," she said reasonably. "I don't mind you putting your name down for anything, but not until you've talked it over with me."

"This doesn't concern you," he said, not harshly.

"Then what the hell are we doing together?" she demanded. "I thought we were special to each other."

"We are, but I knew if I said anything to you, you'd either demand that I give up the idea—"

"Too right! I'm staying too."

"—or try and join me here. Melissa, there's little sense in me being killed, no sense in us both. So you'd better get on the transport and I'll meet you over there in just a few hours. There'll be a transport waiting to pick me up specially after the tornadoes have passed."

"If I get on that plane alone that's the way I'll want it to be. Teld, look supposing you do get killed? What about me?"

"The possibility is extremely remote," Teld replied. "And I wish you'd stop reminding me that it exists. Now you'd better get ready to catch your plane—"

"Oh no," she said. "Like I said, if you're going to risk your neck I'm not passing up the chance to help the noose over your shoulders."

He took a deep breath. "You're not staying—and that's final!"

She stood up and carried the bags wordlessly out into the corridor. Teld looked up at the ceiling and shook his head wonderingly.

CHAPTER ELEVEN

" IF YOU ever tell her it was decided with dice," Teld said, " I'll kill you."

Fourneir smiled and studied the two wooden cubes lying in the palm of his hand. " Of course not," he replied. " I'd never play Fate against itself. I've seen the roll call of those who've lost. Still, it was the only way to find the unlucky member who'd stayed behind. And anyone else would have done the same thing if they'd lost—or won. It's a bit difficult to know what you should say, isn't it? However, I'd better get things ready. The exec. jet'll be here in a few minutes."

" I'll see you over there," Teld said for the second time that day, but less confidently than before. " This thing shouldn't last long. If it's travelling at two miles a minute I make the estimated duration possibly under three minutes."

" But they'll be the worst three minutes of your life," Fourneir promised. " Of course, I wouldn't want you to do this against your wishes, and if it weren't for the only unique aspect of the entire incident, I'd tell Brussels to go hang themselves. Unfortunately—"

" Yes," said Teld. " I know what you mean."

Fourneir slapped his shoulder. " Don't worry she'll be waiting for you. Wouldn't surprise me if she pilots the copter back. I think she holds a licence." He laughed. " I'm only joking, don't worry. But she does seem to have quite a fix on you. And I wouldn't ruin that for either of you."

" Then we'll roll the dice again," Teld suggested.

" Once is good enough for me," Fourneir replied, shaking his head. " I'll see you."

Teld watched him walk across the tarmac and then climb into the waiting aircar. It took off with a burst of speed, scattering dust and loose grit everywhere. The hot, dry, torpid weather seemed to signal the arrival of the storm. He glanced at his watch. He had nine hours left before it struck. Unless a miracle happened between now and then it was inevitable that they should be hit by the maelstrom.

Not long afterwards the last transport clawed its way into the sky and the small jet followed it on the way north. Teld watched it go regretfully, then walked to the garage and climbed into his aircar. It rose and moved forward to the ramp. Once in the sun, he dropped all restrictions and let her have her head.

The exhilarating speed brought his mind back from the small circle it had been treading moments before. Just what were his chances of survival? No one could have told him. And he didn't really want to know.

The aircar picked up speed as it raced toward the perimeter. He didn't bother to look at the clock, but listened to the engine and guessed the speed by the passing of faraway objects. He judged his speed at two fifty when he cut the lift and propulsion turboes.

Without the roar of the engine he could hear the wind screaming in his ears, a long, drawn-out wail which lifted his hair, reminding him of the statue he had seen long ago—it would not be standing now. Well, let it fall. It would have a suitable grave in his mind. The creak of metal stressed, and the heavy wind resistance, forcing him to fight for every breath. He could see the ground coming slowly up to meet the car. There would be no surviving a crash at this speed. A vision of the aircar rolling in flames on the grass of the deserted complex flashed in front of his eyes, so convincing he blinked hard to see whether it had in fact happened. At the same time, without conscious volition, his hand snapped on the lift jets and the sudden thrust upwards bruised every muscle in his body. Why do I keep doing this? he wondered idly. The aircar, without any forward acceleration, soon came to a halt. He waited to recuperate awhile before turning round and heading back towards the Block.

* * *

It was lonelier than he thought it would be. There was no one to talk to, no one to share the pressure with. Mel would possibly be crying and swearing at everyone, at him, and herself in particular. Fourneir would be lambasting whoever was in charge for their cavalier attitude towards the lives of his staff, but it was too late for anyone to fetch him back now. The most he could hope for was the copter Fourneir had promised him, and he sincerely hoped he would be there to meet it.

The first shadow of the storm could be seen on the radar scope. The wallscreen, he had found, could be swung to view the horizon in any direction and he would rely on that for film evidence when the storm arrived. A phrase floated up from the past: 'To learn to ride the unicorn, one must first find a unicorn to ride.' Here the words were especially apt. To study the storm with scientific equipment, you would have to develop equipment able to stand the violence of the storm, while not lessening their sensitivity. On the wallscreen, though, there was nothing to be seen except a dark smudge to the west and the radar hadn't picked up the secondary cell tornadoes. Give them time, he thought, and they'll be round.

He had managed to fall asleep for a couple of hours before dawn and felt reasonably clear-headed after the radar alarm had awoken him. Coffee and biscuits seemed enough for his not particularly demanding stomach. There would be nothing to do now until the computer warned him that the time to leave for the shelter had arrived. Till then, his only thought was to forget the storm, but this proved to be impossible with the evidence waiting for him in front of his eyes. He looked at the smudge on the wallscreen. Was it getting larger? The radar scope showed no trace of the small, destructive tornado groupings.

He wondered what the world would be like several years from now, with the storm having reached its optimum size. Computer projections informed him that the thundercell would circle the globe with high-velocity tornadoes, wrecking in minutes what it had taken men centuries to build. Where would be the best places to survive? On mountains? Or under the seas? There would be very little time to build the necessary homes for enough people to keep the race going.

Certainly none of the major population centres would survive, with the buildings gone and no farms to be worked for food. There might be a possibility they could live in city shelters, as he was doing, but that was not a long-term answer, even to the atom bomb. Besides, eventually the food would run out and they would be forced back to the surface to forage among the ruins. The scope showed that the storm was definitely on its way. He could see the faint spiral shapes of the secondary cell tornado groups as they formed and swept forward towards the Complex. It would be time to leave the Block, for the last time, and find himself a small, dark place in the shelter. He shut off all the systems in the Penthouse, then, after a last look round, travelled up to the ground floor and then out into the sunshine.

There was a strong gale-force wind blowing. He had difficulty keeping his balance against it. Instead of going right to the shelter he walked out on the tarmac to where he could look west and see the storm first hand. Out of the cover of the Block, the winds pulled at him ferociously and it was impossible to look steadily at the black horizon. After a few minutes he found he couldn't move fast enough to counterbalance himself against the gale which threatened to blow him off his feet, so he ran towards the shelter entrance, and sealed the door behind him. Then he switched on the lights and sat down for a while before going on through to the Computer Room, recently put back into working order by technicians, who had also installed a wind-speed recorder and link up with the wallscreen, though both were tenuous contacts indeed and could fail almost any time during the storm. Still, they were both worth having and might make valuable contributions towards the pool of knowledge about the storm.

When the wind speed reached fifty miles an hour he began to record the conditions on tape, and kept a steady eye on the radar scope. The secondary thundercell tornadoes were well into the ephemereal stage now, but he couldn't see whether the tornids had formed yet. And the rate of forward speed was well down now. A nagging suspicion took root. Suppose it didn't move on? Suppose it just centred itself over the Complex and from there on worked out its fate?

He returned to the scope just in time to witness the birth of a tornid. Nothing at first could be seen except a hazy circling on the screen which gradually firmed till the spiral pattern could be made. Before it had finished another circling emerged into being and the cycle was repeated. He measured the distance from the Complex and realised that it was only forty minutes away, if it still travelled at the same speed.

There was little doubt that the tornid had grown since the probe had intercepted it in the Atlantic. The monitor showed the dark forms of the newly-created tornids as they swept down from the hills and mountainsides to touch the valleys. The time was rapidly approaching when he would know whether the shelter was sufficiently sturdy to withstand the fury of the storm.

By this time over half the thundercells were over the mountains and the complement of the CTF was back up to full strength. Behind them, the rear tornadoes were being formed out of the cross winds and charges of the clouds above. He turned to the monitor and searched for the twisters in the distance. When he found them he increased the magnification and looked at the vortices. The funnels wavered to and fro drunkenly, a long black cord reaching up into the sky like the leg of a giant.

His attention drifted back to the Block. Many of the windows had been broken by the wind and a constant shower of broken glass was falling to the ground, the shards glinting like rain in the sun. He remembered that Vortstag would be in the path of the storm, and none of the buildings there would be left standing against the fury. He sighed when he thought of the pleasant afternoon they had spent just outside the bay on one of the boats that would shortly be splinters in a high wind. No doubt there would be other afternoons, but they would be marred by the knowledge of the impending death they couldn't avoid.

The first tornadoes passed just north of the Block sending a shower of debris thrown out by inertial force on to the roof of the shelter. Teld knew there was ten foot of earth over the shelter but the shock could still be felt. Two of the screens on the con died. The radar scope, however, still worked. He could see that the next group would pass directly overhead if they continued on their present course. He gradually became aware of a steady drumming on the roof, random but ceaseless. The topsoil muffled it well, of course . . . but how long would the thin layers stay in place before the winds stripped it away? Originally it had been conceived as an auxiliary particle shield to complement the lead armour of the shelter. Now the particles it would have to cope with would be metal and concrete.

The tornids would not be long behind the groups. They looked very solid on the radar scope, possibly because they would be filled with a constant stream of debris caught up in the funnel. They were still moving sluggishly, but moving inexorably forward all the same.

The thrumming on the roof had become progressively louder over the minutes since it had begun, but now the sound interfered with his concentration. And there didn't appear to be any way of stopping it. This, he thought cynically, was typical of the way things were planned in a hurry. He wasn't in any danger that he could think of, since it would need the roof to crack and the steady downpour of rubble to kill him. Which was extremely unlikely. On the other hand, he could end up with perforated eardrums.

There was an easy way to stop that. In the surgery he found some earplugs and inserted them into his aural cavities. The surgery had everything needed to operate a mini-operating theatre. But with a smile of triumph he returned to the computer room and the tornids.

They had moved on another few miles in the interval but still not as far as had been thought they would. The shelter seemed to move for a moment, and then thumped down with a breath-taking shudder. The lights went out, and for a few moments he was in total darkness. Then the emergency generator picked up, and half-illumination was restored. He realised that the Block must have fallen, or more likely been torn from its foundations by the storm. Whatever had happened the con was now totally useless, with not even the radar scope operating. It was just a dead green circle. He dreaded to think what would happen if the emergency power went.

One factor he couldn't eliminate with the earplugs was the constant vibration the shelter received from the raining debris. Although they could no longer be heard they were most definitely felt. What the storm couldn't pull to pieces, he thought, it would shake to bits. And it would be too much to find that despite all the precautions taken to prevent irradiation he found himself grinning sheepishly from the centre of a pile of shielding.

By his watch the tornids were almost overhead when the noise began to make itself heard through the earplugs. He groaned as the vibration began to produce the sensation of nausea in his stomach. Losing all interest in the Computer Room he staggered out of the swing chair and fell to the floor.

How long he'd been out, he couldn't have said. When

he came to the noise was louder than ever and everything in front of his eyes was an indistinct blur. There would be anti-nausea pills in the surgery, he felt sure. It was impossible to stand upright in these conditions, he soon discovered. He brushed his forehead and his hand came away reddened and tacky. It surprised him that he had been hurt and hadn't felt anything. He would need some antibiotics as well. If he stayed in the Computer Room he would be dead, he was sure of that. The ache in his ears was getting worse and he just couldn't follow his thoughts through.

But there didn't seem to be any place to go, within the shelter. In the surgery he looked around for the medicines but everything was a pile of broken bottles and cabinets on the floor. He finally turned out of the surgery and entered one of the cubicles, closing the door behind him. Groping under the bed he came across an unopened survival kit and swallowed three sedative tabs disregarding the instructions on the packet. Then he pulled the mattress from the bed and crawled to the floor, pulling the cover over him and relaxing. The noise, abated slightly, continued. The sedatives sucked him down towards oblivion as the tornadoes would suck him up to death. In his surrealist thought he could count them, he thought . . . he slept.

* * *

His eyelids fluttered open and he looked out from under the mattress towards the doorway. He groggily got to his feet and removed the earplugs. He still couldn't hear anything, not even his own movements. Things must be really bad, he decided.

The emergency power packs had lasted through the storm and were still providing the necessary life-support systems. He walked into the Computer Room and switched open the doors, then walked out into the Complex and the evening sun.

There was nothing left standing in the whole of his view. The Blocks had both fallen, leaving nothing upright apart from a few inches of wall here and there. In the Computer Block the lift had been drawn out of the shaft by sheer vacuum, leaving a square hole which descended into darkness. One thing which surprised him was the lack of debris. It was as though a cosmic hoover had passed through, clearing everything in its path. He shook his head and returned to the shelter, and took the tapes off their spindles, then carefully packed them in metal cans. He found a pair of field glasses and returned to the surface. The rescue copter was nowhere in sight, which didn't surprise him.

The multipark underground levels were full of cars which had been thrown against one another and now lay as tangled wreckage between the pillars. He discovered several lone cars, but without their keys. Four storeys below ground he finally found one ready for instant travel. As he weaved his way back up to ground level past the crashed vehicles he avoided looking at them.

Vortstag, as he had predicted, was nothing more than a ruined ghost against the sunset. Waves lapped disconsolately against a warped and broken jetty. There were no boats to be found, not even a few pieces of wood drifting on the tide. The storm had taken everything with it.

After circling uselessly the area round Vortstag, hoping to find some other human enclave, he drove back to the Complex, and a few miles from the site of the Blocks saw the black dot settle from the sky on to the ground. He halted the car and looked through the field glasses. They showed the two engined coptor nestled in the grass. As he watched two men emerged from a door in the side, and approached the shelter. He boarded the car and covered the distance in a spectacularly short time.

The men held on to their rifles cautiously while he stood facing them. One moved past him while the other kept cover and examined the canisters in the car seat. Wordlessly he opened them up and lifted the tapes free, then covered them again and motioned to the copter.

"Don't you speak English?" he asked them after the machine had taken off. The guard left him and a few minutes later their superior officer entered the hold of the machine. He too wore a gun strapped on to his flying suit, but smiled at Teld.

"Well done," he said, shaking his hand. "When I heard that we were to look around for someone who had stopped over through that—" he indicated the storm "—I thought you'd either be mad or suicidal. When I heard why, I changed my mind." He looked at Teld for a long while before asking the obvious question. "And was it worth it?" he finally demanded.

The monosyllable took a lot from him, but it relieved

the insane pressure that he felt had been building up on his brain. When he delivered the verdict on a world, he did so without emotion, and without apparent concern.

"No," he said.